SHERLOCK HOLMES

AND THE
UNHOLY TRINITY

By the same author

The Lost Files of Sherlock Holmes
The Chronicles of Sherlock Holmes
Sherlock Holmes and the Giant Rat of Sumatra
The Annals of Sherlock Holmes

SHERLOCK HOLMES

AND THE

UNHOLY TRINITY

PAUL D. GILBERT

ROBERT HALE · LONDON

© Paul D. Gilbert 2015

First published in Great Britain 2015

ISBN 978-0-7198-1300-9

Robert Hale Limited
Clerkenwell House
Clerkenwell Green
London EC1R 0HT

www.halebooks.com

2 4 6 8 10 9 7 5 3 1

Typeset in Palatino
Printed in Great Britain by Berforts Information Press Ltd.

CONTENTS

Introduction   7

PART ONE

The Death of Cardinal Tosca

'His famous investigation into the sudden death of
Cardinal Tosca, an inquiry that was carried out by him
at the express desire of His Holiness the Pope.'

From *The Adventure of Black Peter* by A.C.D.

Chapter One: An Unexpected Visitor   11

Chapter Two: An Unexpected Request   21

Chapter Three: We Return to Rome   27

Chapter Four: Inspector Gialli   31

Chapter Five: At Last … A Clue!   40

Chapter Six: An Audience   54

Chapter Seven: A Wire to Mrs Hudson   59

PART TWO

The Coptic Patriarchs

'You know that I am preoccupied with the case of the two Coptic Patriarchs, which should come to a head today.'

From *The Adventure of the Retired Colourman* by A.C.D.

Chapter Eight: The Cradle of Civilization 73

Chapter Nine: A Sacred Ally 86

Chapter Ten: The Last of the Few 99

Chapter Eleven: Flight from Egypt 115

Chapter Twelve: The Unholy Trinity 138

Chapter Thirteen: Our Journey Home 155

Chapter Fourteen: Inspector Lestrade 166

Chapter Fifteen: The Diogenes Club 190

Chapter Sixteen: The Final Resolution 206

Notes 224

INTRODUCTION

O NCE I HAD completed my last book, *The Annals of Sherlock Holmes*, I was left convinced that I had exhausted each one of the teaser references that Conan Doyle had enticingly inserted within his great works.

However, on closer examination of some of his lesser known stories, I realized that there were still two potential gems that required closer examination. Not only that, but they seemed to lend themselves to each other in a way that I found to be utterly irresistible. I do hope that you and Sir Arthur will excuse this further indulgence of mine and I trust that you will find them as intriguing as I have done.

It has been a thrill for me to be able to bring these marvellous characters back to life once more. Not for the first time, I must thank my partner in crime and ever tolerant wife, Jackie, for her invaluable support and advice.

P.D.G.

PART ONE

THE DEATH OF
CARDINAL TOSCA

CHAPTER ONE

AN UNEXPECTED VISITOR

MARCH 6 1896 is a date that will certainly live long, if not perpetually, within my memory.

For this was the day on which Sherlock Holmes and I had thrust upon us the outset of one of the most remarkable and dramatic adventures that we had ever experienced. Furthermore, it was one that very nearly cost us both our lives!

We were on the point of concluding a most quiet and leisurely breakfast. Holmes had already filled his customary first pipe of the day. This normally consisted of a collection of all the plugs and dottles from his previous day's smokes that he had accumulated upon the top of the mantelpiece.

He had filled his old brier pipe and was on the point of putting a match to this pungent concoction when we were both alerted to a tremendous commotion coming from the hallway below. There was a scream of terror emanating from our long-suffering landlady, Mrs Hudson.

The stairway seemed to quake beneath the feet of what sounded like a thousand men and an instant later the door to our rooms was sent crashing from its hinges by a force of seismic proportions! Holmes and I barely had enough time to jump out of our seats, much less to prepare ourselves for a confrontation. There before us stood a most imposing and decidedly hostile individual the like of which I had only ever encountered within the pages of the *National Geographic*.

The shattered remnants of our door revealed a veritable giant of a man who was bedecked in the traditional garb of the legendary desert Bedouin. His dress was replete with a dashing, flowing cloak, swirling and colourful robes and his headwear and waist sash were decorated with shimmering gold and lustrous gems.

However, our attention had been immediately diverted away from this splendour and instead directed towards the enormous sword that the Bedouin now brandished within his right hand. With a surprising lack of effort and with a speed that belied the size of both the man and his ferocious weapon, the Bedouin had unsheathed an intricately decorated curved blade, known as a Shamshir. Mercifully, the threatening appearance of this sword was deadlier than the intent of its bearer.

'Beware of the dangers of interfering with matters that are surely no concern of yours, Mr Holmes! We warn you now, stay out of our affairs or risk facing the fatal consequences of your actions!' The giant issued his dramatic warning in surprisingly good English and with a voice that boomed from the very bowels of the earth.

Holmes and I were rooted to the spot. My first instinct was to move as far away as possible from the imposing Bedouin. I backed away slowly towards the window and looked towards Holmes for guidance.

To my dismay and despite the very obvious threat to his life that was being posed by our loud and extravagant guest, Holmes clapped his hands repeatedly and then burst into a peel of strident laughter!

'Well, I must say, you certainly know how to put on a very

entertaining show indeed!' Holmes exclaimed.

The Bedouin reddened with rage and frustration. Then, as if to demonstrate that his initial threat had been no idle display, he raised the Shamshir above his head and glared at Holmes with as much anger and hatred as I had ever witnessed. He then brought the blade down upon the very chair that I had been sitting on but a moment before!

Such had been the ferocity of the blow and the trueness of the blade that the solid oak had been cleaved clean through without having caused but a handful of splinters. The chair then collapsed onto the floor, in two equal parts, before it was the turn of the Bedouin to laugh.

'I beseech you, Mr Holmes, do not make light of my warning.' He shook his head slowly. 'This time it is only the chair.' There was menace in the way that his voice had now dropped to the merest whisper.

The Bedouin then sheathed his weapon with a dramatic flourish; he turned on his heels and marched purposely from our rooms. Another gut-wrenching cry from Mrs Hudson announced his arrival upon the lower landing and a staggering vibration, throughout the entire building, confirmed his violent departure from 221b Baker Street.

'Well, upon my word! Holmes, you really must be more selective as to whom you mock and laugh at,' I said reproachfully.

I might as well have saved myself the effort for all the effect that it had on Holmes, for he appeared to be undaunted by the entire episode! He rubbed his hands gleefully together as he contemplated the prospect of a new adventure.

'Well, Watson, our impromptu visitor certainly added some much-needed zest to what was otherwise a rather mundane little meal,' Holmes suggested mischievously.

'It was more than a little zest that cleaved my chair in two!' I protested. 'I am also more than a bit surprised that, once again, you have thought it necessary to exclude me from your confidence.'

'Whatever can you mean?' Holmes asked of me with an air of amused curiosity.

'Oh, come along, Holmes, you cannot expect me to believe, for one instant, that you are ignorant of the motive behind the display of violence that we have just witnessed,' I insisted.

So often had Holmes appeared to be a man bereft of all normal human emotion, that I took some satisfaction from observing a slight tremor in his fingers when he lit a cigarette.

'I can assure you, Watson, that apart from the obvious results of my rudimentary observation, my knowledge of our colourful visitor is as scant as your own.' I must confess that Holmes's reply did appear to have been a sincere one.

'Well, then, why did he seem to direct all of his threats and attention towards you alone? Surely you would have recognized, at once, any attempt that such an individual might have made in identifying you? Yet not once did he acknowledge my presence, even with a passing glance,' I reasoned, although by now my tone had lost its reproachful edge.

'Perhaps a less obtrusive colleague of his has been keeping me under a discreet surveillance?' Holmes suggested thoughtfully.

'So you have already reached the conclusion that our visitor is not operating as an individual.' I regretted having made this remark before the words had even left my lips. Not surprisingly, Holmes turned on me without a moment's hesitation.

'Watson, surely not even you could have failed to have noticed his use of the phrases "we warn you" and "our affairs"? There should be no doubt in your mind, therefore, that we have ruffled the feathers of a very dangerous group of conspirators, albeit inadvertently. Perhaps any reputation that I might have accrued has now become something of a liability.'

Holmes turned to me, baring a malevolent grimace that quite took me aback.

'Your lamentably romanticized depiction of my more recent successes and the over-enthusiastic coverage of the press that has resulted from them has certainly done nothing to dampen the public's appetite for such things ... to their shame! Consequently, as a direct result of the poisoned chalice of my fame, our enthusiastic visitor has assumed my involvement in his affair before the facts.'

Holmes's chain of thoughts had certainly resulted in his falling into one of his dark and irritable moods and I recognized at once the futility of my offering any kind of defence for the innocence of my humble literary offerings. I displayed my displeasure by picking up a fragment of my chair and then dashing it petulantly to the floor.

I realized that this gesture of mine had gone unnoticed when I observed Holmes violently rummaging through the pile of untouched morning papers that had been piled high upon the dining table.

'Quickly, Watson, there is not a moment to lose!' He threw some of the papers towards me and we began to scour them for any reference to our visitor and his associations. Page by page the papers were being rejected and Holmes hurled them carelessly and chaotically to the floor where they began to form a haphazard carpet of print.

I was being more deliberate with my examinations than was my friend and he soon became impatient and irritated at my lack of progress. Holmes snatched the offending papers from my grasp and his eyes fell at once upon the article that had been occupying my attention. The sensational headline highlighted a most brutal murder that had taken place, the night before, in the suburb of Dagenham.

'Really, Watson, we have no time to spare upon such a commonplace little incident. It is fairly obvious, even from these scant lines, that the gardener carried out the killing with his shovel!' Before I could chastise him for having made so bold and outrageous an assertion, Holmes added the paper to the mayhem on the floor.

With a most unfortunate sense of timing, it was at this precise moment that our ashen-faced and bewildered land-lady shuffled slowly into the room. Her eyes moved in disbelief from the door to the chair and they finally rested upon my friend as he continued to defile the best that Fleet Street had to offer. Mrs Hudson was so taken aback by the sight that she was incapable of making a single utterance.

'Quickly, Watson, I fear that Mrs Hudson is about to faint!' Holmes called out urgently.

I dropped yet another newspaper to the floor and imme-diately reached out to support the poor woman by her shoulders, barely an instant before her legs gave way from beneath her. I ushered her gently over to my armchair by the fire. Once I was satisfied that she was comfortably and securely seated, I ran to fetch some salts from my bag and administered them to her without a moment's delay.

The effects of the salts were both immediate and a little disconcerting. The colour soon returned to Mrs Hudson's cheeks and she glared ferociously towards Holmes, who was now standing rather sheepishly by the window.

'Mr Holmes,' she scolded rather hoarsely. 'You are, without a doubt, the worst and the most dangerous tenant that has ever lived!'

Holmes immediately activated his most charming of smiles and his voice adopted the smoothest of tones.

'My most humble apologies, Mrs Hudson, and I assure you that I shall put matters to right in no time at all. Dr Watson here will confirm that I have a rather substantial remunera-tion coming my way for services rendered to the Dutch royal family. I assure you that the door and chair will soon be as good as new. As for the newspapers ...'

Holmes dropped to the floor and began to gather up the offending journals into a neat pile. He presented this to Mrs Hudson while remaining humbly on his knees. Mrs Hudson visibly warmed to Holmes's charming gesture and she could not help but smile at him as he slowly stood up while still clutching the newspapers.

'Thank you once again, Mrs Hudson, for your kindness and many considerations. If it is any consolation or comfort to you, I can assure you that I am totally ignorant as to the identity of our most singular visitor and his reason for coming here this morning,' Holmes added.

Mrs Hudson was walking towards the door with a good deal more certainty than when she had first entered the room. She stopped suddenly and turned back towards us with steely intent.

'No, Mr Holmes, it is of no consolation whatsoever!' she stated simply and then she proceeded through the remains of the door and back towards the stairs.

Holmes attempted to close the door behind our tormented landlady, although all he succeeded in doing was to render its attachment to the frame as even more precarious. He abandoned the door to its fate and decided to join me by the fire with a pipe. His choice of the cherry wood seemed to indicate that he was in a contemplative mood and we sat in thoughtful silence for a while.

'So, Watson, what then are we to make of this morning's little interlude?' Holmes turned to me suddenly. I could not help but smile at his unexpected turn of phrase; however, when I looked across at him I soon recognized that he was in deadly earnest.

'Well,' I began uncertainly, 'we seem to know very little about the brute but still less about the motives behind his threatening behaviour towards you. I presume that we must now simply await further developments,' I concluded lamely, at a loss for any alternative course of action.

'No, Watson, we must be able to do better than that!' Holmes exclaimed. 'If an unknown party has somehow managed to implicate me in the affairs of the swordsman and his confederates, I have no intention of simply sitting in our rooms and awaiting the next attack! As the fellow so eloquently put it, next time it may not be just a chair that feels the force of his fearsome blow.'

'Then kindly explain to me what other measures are available to us? As you have said, on many separate occasions, it is pointless to speculate without possessing the facts,' I insisted.

'That much is true, Watson. However, I can assure you that I acquired enough knowledge of the man, even from so brief an observation, that will enable me to send off two wires, confident in receiving one successful reply at the very least!'

I was left irritated at my own ineptitude by Holmes's inscrutable reply. I had not the slightest notion as to what Holmes had been referring and I was resigned to having to prise this information from him, or remain in ignorance until a time that suited him.

Holmes seemed to sense this and for once, and to my great surprise, he decided to share his thoughts with me without my having to coerce them from him first. He abandoned his cherry wood and moved over to the window with a lighted cigarette.

He presented me with his sharply defined profile and the dim light, which was cast through the grimy glass of the window, surrounded his features with an indistinct halo that caused me to imagine him as some kind of esoteric font of sublime knowledge. I was in little doubt that this had certainly been his intention for, as always, he found a dramatic flourish irresistible.

A hurried change of heart saw him return to the table

whereupon he scribbled out the two wires to which he had just alluded. Once he had despatched them, by way of a pale and reluctant Mrs Hudson, I felt sure that he might now be ready to discuss things fully.

'Might I ask as to the contents of those wires and their intended recipients?' I broached the subject tentatively.

'That is a most excellent idea, Watson!' He shot me the briefest of smiles before continuing. 'This could prove to be a most meritorious exercise if you are to formulate an intelligent appraisal of events, which might then aid me in my investigations.' Holmes returned to his chair by the fire before he continued.

'Doubtless you might not be surprised to hear that I have wired my old friend and colleague, Inspector Berlajous of the Paris Gendarmerie. He has long been a dedicated if not inspired disciple of my method and he maintains a most scrutinized eye upon the area of his jurisdiction. The identity of the other recipient may not be so obvious to you; it is none other than Elraji of the constabulary of Port Said!' Holmes concluded with a flourish that implied that he considered no other explanation was necessary.

I must have been considerably less than successful in concealing an expression of perplexed confusion than I had hoped, for Holmes was evidently much amused by my bewilderment. He shook his head slowly in disappointment.

'Really, Watson, despite our friend's masterful grasp of our mother tongue, you could not have failed to recognize a light Gallic lilt at the conclusion of each of his sentences? That he has not long been in this country is evident from his attire. He has clearly made no concession for our harsh equinoctial March winds! He obviously arrived at Baker Street by cab, for despite this morning's continuous downpour, his silk robes only bore a few blemishes from the rain.'

Clearly warming to his task, Holmes continued in a state

of some excitement and leant forward whilst balancing his elbows precariously upon his bony knees.

'Since the only boat train at Victoria Station this morning was scheduled to arrive at no more than thirty minutes before the Bedouin made his entrance, it is obvious that he began his journey from the Gallic side of the English Channel!' Holmes held out his arms theatrically, as if he had just performed a remarkable feat of magic, which, in one sense, he just had.

This rapid and remarkable explanation had left me feeling quite breathless and it was a moment or two before I was able to ask him to explain the wire to Elraji. I was on the point of doing so when Mrs Hudson burst excitedly into the room.

'Excuse me, gentlemen, but this urgent message has just been pushed into my hands. The postmark is from Rome!'

CHAPTER TWO

AN UNEXPECTED REQUEST

HOLMES WAS OUT of his chair in an instant and in a single bound he arrived at Mrs Hudson's side, whereupon he slipped the wire from her fingers.

'Thank you, Mrs Hudson.' Holmes quietly ushered her from the room while he tossed the wire towards me with a flourish. 'Please, Watson, if you would be so kind.'

I tore the communication open with a feverish excitement for it bore the unmistakable red, gold, cross-keys crest of the Holy See! Holmes calmly took up a cross-legged position on his armchair while he closed his eyes in a state of serene concentration.

The wire was scant in detail but dramatic in content. Acting on behalf of His Holiness the Pope, Cardinal Pietro, his closest confidante, formally requested Holmes's assistance in the investigation of the tragic and mysterious death of his friend and colleague, Cardinal Tosca! Due to the extreme delicacy of the matter, Cardinal Pietro had requested both a discreet and prompt inquiry and he consequently requested a reply by return. If Holmes would forward the projected time of his arrival he would be met at the terminus by Inspector

Gialli of the Polizia of Rome.

Holmes continued to sit in silence for a few moments. When his eyes finally reopened they were alive with the blaze of excitement that I had previously witnessed on many such occasions. He sprang from his chair and over to the fireplace, rubbing his hands together by the fire.

'So, Watson, what are we to make of this intriguing petition? Although it is scant on detail it does seem to present us with a number of interesting possibilities, would you not say?'

I could barely suppress my amusement at Holmes's exaggerated understatement.

'I am surprised that you have even hesitated for this long!' I exclaimed. 'After all, a summons from the Roman Pontiff himself is hardly an everyday occurrence. A murder in the Vatican and the opportunity to renew your acquaintance with the redoubtable Inspector Gialli must surely be irresistible to you?'

'Indeed, but what say you, Watson, to such an undertaking? After all, you have already made the assumption that we would be investigating a case of murder. Surely you know of my aversion to making assumptions prior to possessing the relevant facts?' Holmes added reproachfully.

'Oh, come along, Holmes, my assumption is hardly stretching the bounds of imagination to its limits! A reference to tragic and mysterious circumstances does not imply that Cardinal Tosca choked to death on a chicken bone! As to my own involvement, well, all I can say is that if my presence would not be too much of an encumbrance, I could be back here, with a packed bag and my army revolver at the ready, within an hour,' I pledged.

Holmes clapped his hands together delightedly.

'Well said, friend Watson! Be assured that your companionship would be of immeasurable benefit to me in the Eternal City. As for it being a murder investigation, I cannot flaw even one word of your incisive hypothesis! By the time of your return, I shall have put our *Bradshaw* to most excellent use and have a reply to Cardinal Pietro winging towards the Vatican with all due haste.'

Holmes was already rummaging through the pages of that well-thumbed volume before I had even passed through our shattered threshold. However, upon my return, I was dismayed to see that my friend was now slumped back into his chair wearing a most crestfallen demeanour, with our *Bradshaw* strewn forlornly upon the floor at his feet. I put down the belongings, which I had raised so triumphantly upon entering the room, and immediately enquired as to the cause of his sudden change of mood.

'Alas, Watson, *Bradshaw* indicates that there will not be another boat train to Boulogne until ten o'clock tomorrow morning.' He emitted a grunt of disapproval while he began to strum his fingers upon the arm of his chair at a most alarming tempo.

'Surely that schedule does not present us with too much of a dilemma?' I suggested by way of consolation. 'I can surely use my old room for the night and we shall even be afforded sufficient time for a light breakfast before our departure.'

'What use do I have for breakfast?' Holmes snapped angrily. 'All the while that our journey is delayed, the trail in Rome grows ever colder and the greater becomes the risk of valuable clues becoming obscured by carelessness or ineptitude!'

'Surely our old friend Inspector Gialli[1] would not allow affairs to reach such a sorry pass?' I responded reassuringly.

'I suppose you are right, Watson.' Holmes smiled begrudgingly. 'I can assure you, however, that if Gialli's Scotland Yard counterparts happened to be involved I would hardly be filled with the same confidence!' Holmes leapt to his feet and immediately despatched a wire to the Vatican with our revised time of arrival at the terminus of Rome.

The evening that we spent together was reminiscent of the many that we had spent in like fashion during my permanent residency at 221b Baker Street. Mrs Hudson was only too pleased to extend the light supper to my plate and once the remains had been removed, Holmes and I took to our chairs by the fireside with our pipes and a glass of a rather excellent port.

Holmes entertained me with a delightful rendition of Beethoven's violin concerto and not a mention was made of the rousing adventure that undoubtedly lay before us. I decided that an early night was in order, but as I left Holmes to his pipes, I found it impossible to speculate as to the thoughts that he was harbouring behind his steely and deter-mined countenance. Nevertheless, I felt certain that he would not rest for an instant until he had ensured that justice would eventually prevail.

I spent a restless night upon my old bed, in my old room. I wasted many hours of valuable sleep by indulging in fruit-less speculation upon the events and adventures that would undoubtedly lie ahead of us. I had no misgivings about undertaking such an adventure by my friend's side. I had left my surgery within the safe hands of Dr Farquar, a colleague and neighbour who had assisted me in this way on many such occasions. My affairs were in good order and I was free to assist Holmes in any manner that might be required.

However, I could not lay easy. The thrill that would nor-mally have gripped me on the eve of such an adventure had been supplanted by an inexplicable sense of dread and fore-boding. Perhaps my subconscious mind was reminding me of the reason behind our previous visit to the Eternal City. A single word now reverberated around the inside of my head. Moriarty!

Although I had not been aware of his involvement at the time of our departure, by the time that we had reached Rome,

Holmes had left me in little doubt that Moriarty had been the mastermind behind the daring and ingenious theft of that brilliant, classical piece of sculpture, 'The Dying Gaul', from the Capitoline Museums.

Of course, I was not so befuddled by my lack of sleep that the notion of Moriarty's involvement, on this occasion, had ever crossed my mind. After all, I had been present at the time of his final demise and even he was not capable of such a phenomenon! Nonetheless, his name alone was enough to deny me of a restful night.

I abandoned my bed, poured out a glass of water from my carafe and lit a cigarette. As I sat by my open window, my mind went back to the penultimate and longest stage of our previous journey to Rome, namely the stretch that had taken us by train from Paris to Turin. It was at this point that Holmes had decided to divulge to me a secret that he had been harbouring for nigh on four years: Professor Moriarty was still alive.

My immediate reaction had been one of concern for my friend's state of mind, so outlandish had seemed this assertion of his to me. However, as the miles continued to flash past our windows, Holmes outlined to me a process of thought and deduction that had been so sublime in its clarity and pure logic, that by its conclusion I had been left in no doubt that it had been Moriarty's brother, the Colonel, who had perished at Holmes's hand at the falls of Reichenbach and not the Professor.

Holmes's demonstration had been so enthralling that our arrival at Turin felt premature in the extreme and all thoughts of my friend's instability had been long abandoned.

My reminiscences left me exhausted and by the time I had extinguished my cigarette and closed the window, I was all but asleep.

It seemed like only the briefest of moments had passed

before I felt my shoulder being prodded by a set of long, bony fingers, although it was, in truth, already seven o'clock the following morning. My bleary eyes could just make out the sight of Sherlock Holmes smiling eagerly down at me.

'Watson,' he said quietly. 'The journey begins!'

CHAPTER THREE

WE RETURN TO ROME

As it transpired, we did, indeed, have time for a light but most welcomed breakfast before our departure from Baker Street.

Our stalwart ally and undoubtedly the finest cabby ever to drive upon the streets of London, Dave 'Gunner' King, pulled up outside 221b at exactly the appointed time and after a few brief words of consolation and farewell to Mrs Hudson, we boarded the cab.

The shortest stage of our long journey seemed to be all the briefer as King used all of his skill and knowledge to get us to Charing Cross well ahead of our schedule. As we flew along those familiar streets I could only wonder how long it would be before we were to do so again. Then a thought occurred to me.

'Holmes, you have always voiced your reluctance to leave London for any length of time, fearing that the criminal classes were likely to run amok during your absence. What has caused you to alter your opinion in this instance?' I asked quietly.

'Sadly, Watson, the age of the master criminal is now a

thing of the past. As any student of your lamentable chronicles of my work will attest to, our more recent cases have been somewhat less than stimulating. Indeed, it is only your habit of embellishing the truth with a liberal smattering of contemporary and romantic sensationalism that has made them almost readable. On that basis I am certain that the resolute Inspector Lestrade and his cohorts are well able to maintain some degree of control ... at least until my return!'

I smiled at my friend's inability to conceal an air of neither superiority nor any conceit from his voice and I could detect no humour in his demeanour whatsoever.

'I assure you, Watson, that we will be dealing with issues far graver than any that either of us can possibly imagine. It would be against my nature if I were to pass up an opportunity such as this for the sake of neither a petty piece of larceny nor a sordid little murder. Let Scotland Yard feast upon these while they may! Hah, Charing Cross already, well done, King!' Holmes called up to our driver while we got down our luggage.

The crossing to Boulogne passed without incident and Holmes and I enjoyed a bracing walk around the upper deck of the ferry. However, when we finally reached our destination we were frustrated to learn that the line to Paris was under overnight repair. Holmes immediately sent a further message to Inspector Gialli, to warn him of our delay, and he beseeched him to ensure that nothing be removed from Cardinal Tosca's office prior to our arrival.

At least I had the consolation of being able to spend a delightful afternoon and evening in that charming sea port and we found that the local wine and seafood was exceptional.

Holmes, of course, was not so easily consoled and he spent much of our time in Boulogne pacing relentlessly around the harbour, forever fretting over the potential loss of clues that our continued delay might have been bringing about. He was oblivious to the town's delights and he was smoking his cigarettes at an alarming rate. However, I was at least able to persuade him to partake of a bowl of most excellent bisque and a carafe of local wine, which seemed to settle his nerves somewhat.

Holmes was so intent on ensuring that we suffered no further delays that we found ourselves at the station a full hour before our scheduled departure time. Sadly, for me at any rate, it meant that we had to forgo the delights of our hotel's breakfast menu.

We barely had time to make our connection once we did reach Paris and as a consequence it was almost lunchtime before any food had passed our lips. I was disappointed to discover that the buffet car was woefully inadequate and we had returned to our seats and our pipes within a very short time of leaving them.

The longest stretch of our journey now lay ahead of us and I could not help but recall the last time we had travelled from Paris to Turin. On this occasion we were travelling through the night so once again I was denied the opportunity to enjoy the spectacular Tuscan landscapes that we were now passing through.

Of course, on the previous journey Holmes had mesmerized me with his wondrous dissection of the dramatic events that had supposedly occurred atop of the Reichenbach Falls in 1891. This time we were being lured to Rome by a set of circumstances that were certainly no less significant than those that had led us to the Eternal City previously. I was surprised to note, therefore, that Holmes had barely uttered a word since our departure from the Gallic capital.

'I apologize for not being able to enlighten and entertain you this time, Watson,' Holmes said suddenly, almost as if he had been able to read my innermost thoughts.

I could not help but laugh at this further display of Holmes's insightfulness.

'Well, upon my word, Holmes, does nothing ever escape you?' I exclaimed.

'I may seem to be oblivious to my surroundings at times, but my sense of awareness is always active and acute. It has not escaped my notice that it was at this stage of our previous journey that I decided to break my silence upon the matter of the Moriarty brothers.

'Your frequent and furtive glances in my direction indicated to me that you were equally aware of the significance of our surroundings and hopeful of further shocking revelations. I am afraid, however, that it will be some time before they will be forthcoming ... but they will come,' Holmes added emphatically and enigmatically.

As Holmes spoke these last few words I felt the thrill of excitement coursing through me, because Holmes was not a man who ever spoke idly. For once, however, the nature of these revelations was as much of a mystery to Holmes as they were to me and they were likely to remain so until our investigations in Rome finally began.

'We shall have to rely on Inspector Gialli a good deal more than when we looked into the matter of "The Dying Gaul",' Holmes stated rather surprisingly. 'These are far deeper and darker waters than any that we have previously encountered, Watson, and Gialli's knowledge and thoroughness will prove to be invaluable to us.'

'That is not to mention his obvious linguistic advantages,' I added. I recalled how by the end of the earlier case Holmes and Gialli had formed an unusual bond of mutual respect and I could sense that Holmes was actually rather looking forward to working alongside the dapper little Italian once again.

At this point I could see that Holmes had lapsed into one of his long circumspective silences once more and before too long I sank into the back of my seat and fell into a deep, though restless sleep.

CHAPTER FOUR

INSPECTOR GIALLI

I WAS AWAKE long before we pulled into the bustling station of Turin and I found Holmes smiling patronizingly down at me as I rubbed my eyes.

'So, Watson, I see that you have finally decided to rejoin the land of the living!' Holmes greeted me with surprising cheerfulness. 'We still have some little time before we arrive at Turin and, unless my memory has failed me, this train provides an above average buffet car.'

'A late supper would suit me admirably,' I responded with some surprise in my voice. It was unusual in the extreme for Holmes to instigate a proposal of food and on the eve of a new adventure, almost unthinkable. He had discovered long ago that the energy required for the digestion of food could be best spent upon the case at hand.

Evidently the anticipation of the intriguing nature of the adventure that lay ahead of us, together with the eminent and pious persona of our client, had activated Holmes's dormant appetite. He dwelt upon the menu for but the briefest of moments and gave his order.

'The last time that we made this journey, you enlisted my

assistance under false pretences,' I began and then, in anticipation of Holmes's protests, I continued without drawing
breath. 'You decided to wait until we had reached this exact
point before you condescended to outline to me your theories
regarding Professor Moriarty. Evidently you have decided to
manipulate me in a similar fashion, once again,' I concluded.

'My dear Watson, whatever can you possibly mean?'
Holmes eyed me quizzically but he could not disguise his
amusement at my bold statement.

'Oh, come along, Holmes, how often have you been so
keen to take a meal on the eve of a new case? It seems obvious
to me that you possess more information than you have
divulged to me so far,' I protested.

'Watson, you really should refrain from speculation and
theorizing until such time as you have accumulated sufficient
data to substantiate those theories. Nevertheless, there is an
element of truth in what you say.'

To my great chagrin, it was at this moment that our food
arrived and Holmes waved aside any thoughts of further
discussion until our meal was concluded. As our train rolled
on sedately through the night, Holmes and I lingered over
our impromptu late supper, to the point where I became
convinced that he was deliberately prevaricating. Finally,
however, Holmes picked up his glass of port and his cigar
and I eagerly followed him out onto the observation carriage.

We drank and smoked in silence for a while and I was
surprised to note how much quieter the engine sounded
from this, the furthest extremity of the train. The landscape
appeared as nothing more than a rolling bank of immovable
dark shadows but the night sky was clear of cloud and I had
no great difficulty in identifying my old friend 'The Great
Bear'. I would have pointed out this observation to my friend
but, as you might recall, his knowledge of astronomy was
somewhat less than basic!

Once again Holmes broke in upon my innermost thoughts.

'Watson, you must realize that the stars and their constellations are of no more relevance to my work than the name of the King of Siam! It is a capital error to mistake discrimination for ignorance. I am a slave to my work and I only employ the tools that are best suited to the desired result. Nevertheless, even I could not have failed to recognize "The Great Bear"!' Holmes exclaimed jovially.

'Well, I am certainly glad to hear you say that, perhaps now you would explain to me which aspect of my theory you consider to be correct?'

'I give you my assurance, Watson, that your reason for accompanying me is absolutely genuine and I would never consider deceiving you again unless it was absolutely necessary. However, it has occurred to me that we may be investigating not one but two distinct mysteries, although they are obviously interrelated.'

'Two mysteries?' I repeated while slowly shaking my head. 'I am sorry, but I simply do not understand.'

'I should have recognized this from the outset, indeed from the very moment that you read out the wire from Cardinal Pietro. Consider, if you will, the use of the words "delicacy" and "discreet". Given those two criteria, the question is, why did they send for me?' Holmes asked rather surprisingly.

'Why, Holmes, surely there is no great mystery there! After all, your successful recovery of "The Dying Gaul" is very well documented and obviously His Holiness wished to call upon the very best.'

'Whilst your flattery is very gratifying, Watson, you must realize that it is because of your lamentable journals and the sensational reputation of the original crime that Gialli and I have achieved a form of local celebrity. That is hardly the backdrop for a discreet inquiry.'

'Perhaps not, Holmes, but surely you will agree that there

33

are grounds to suppose that the inquiry will prove to be a successful one.'

Holmes considered silently for a moment while he finished his cigar.

'No, no, no,' Holmes repeated slowly and quietly. 'The first crime was a civil one whilst this time we are dealing with a secular matter. Do not forget that the Vatican is an autonomous city state and as such they have their own set of modus operandi.

'It is surprising in itself that they have breached their walls enough to bring in Inspector Gialli, but to ask for my assistance as well is unthinkable under the circumstances. I fear that there are darker forces abroad here than we previously imagined. We must tread a very light foot forward, Watson, from this point onwards,' Holmes concluded solemnly.

I could not think of a single word to offer in counter argument and Holmes's inference had a decidedly disquieting effect upon me. Neither of us offered another word upon the subject and we decided to retire for what little remained of the night.

The change of trains at Turin proved to be quite effortless and we arrived at the terminus of Rome nearly thirty hours after our departure from Baker Street. Even though the delay in Paris had extended our journey by a good six hours, we were impressed to discover that Inspector Gialli was awaiting our arrival with a fine landau drawn by two pairs.

Gialli was clearly excited at the prospect of working with us once again for he leapt down from the carriage to greet us with a broad smile and a cheery wave. We returned his enthusiastic greeting and before long we were making a slow and sedate progress towards our hotel which was situated upon the Via Nazionale.

It was only now, with Gialli seated directly opposite to me, that I was able to recognize certain fundamental alterations in the inspector's appearance and mannerisms. Whilst it was true to say that his short rotund physique was as dapper as ever in his light grey mohair suit, I could not help but notice an uncharacteristic nervous trembling in his left leg.

The elegance of his hat and cane were now offset by his uneven moustache and a two-day stubble. His calm, organized comportment was marred by a constant scowl and an anxious, unnatural smile that made me feel quite uneasy.

I speculated as to the cause of these changes. Perhaps the burden of the current case and the prestigious location of the crime were exerting too many demands upon his narrow shoulders? Of course, it was also possible that my perception of the man had become clouded by the passage of time. That seemed hardly likely, however, as the case of 'The Dying Gaul' had been only two years ago.

Before I was able to conclude my rustic analysis, Gialli pulled out his notebook and began a brief outline of the case so far. I had been so distracted by Gialli's appearance and his behaviour that Holmes had to motion for me to follow suit. For the sake of a smooth narrative, I have erased all traces of Gialli's accent and tendency towards mispronunciation.

'Signor Holmes, despite the grotesque nature of the crime, the bare facts of the case are as unambiguous as one could hope for. Two days ago, while seated at his office desk, Cardinal Tosca had his throat slit from ear to ear by someone wielding a large curved blade.'

'Upon my word!' I exclaimed. 'How awful!' Holmes appeared to be unmoved by this revelation and merely repeated his instruction that I should begin to fill my notebook.

'Indeed, Doctor Watson,' Gialli confirmed with an emphatic nod of his head.

'You are certain of the nature of this weapon?' Holmes

asked quietly.

'Absolutely, Signor Holmes, the shape of the wound is unmistakable and this is confirmed by the outline of the incision in the window where it had been forced open. Of course, the weapon had disappeared with the intruder, although it is evident to me that he had been interrupted and quite abruptly.'

Holmes turned towards the inspector whilst wearing a look of amused admiration.

'Really, Inspector, please explain to me how you can be so certain of this.'

'It is because of the position of the parchment in relation to the pool of blood from Cardinal Tosca's wound—'

'I am sorry, I do not understand.' I found it impossible to continue with my notes without interrupting Gialli in full flow.

'No need to apologize, Doctor Watson, I will explain my meaning. I have it on good authority, from one of the cardinal's secretaries, that he had been studying an ancient piece of parchment, almost continuously, from the moment that it had arrived on his desk three days earlier. The parchment had been delivered by a courier from Egypt and had created great excitement within the halls of the Vatican. You can imagine that a wound such as he had suffered would have bled most profusely.'

'Oh, without a doubt,' I confirmed. 'The carotids are two of our main arteries and are positioned on each side of the throat.' Holmes nodded as I demonstrated with a finger on my own throat.

'Yet the parchment, which the cardinal had been working over for the best part of seventy-two hours, had barely suffered even a speckle of blood!' Gialli exclaimed. 'To me the implication of this anomaly is quite clear. The intruder came with the express intention of removing the parchment and he was in the process of doing so when he struck his fatal blow. Obviously the timely intervention of a member of the Swiss Guard forced him to leave without his coveted prize.'

'That was a brilliant piece of deduction, Inspector,' I stated admiringly, but my friend did not appear to be so convinced. He also congratulated Gialli yet I could tell from his faraway manner and the deep pursing of his lips with his forefinger that his words were empty and that he felt that Gialli's analysis was open to an entirely different interpretation. I was certain that I would not be privy to Holmes's version of events until his investigation was well underway.

We sat in silence for a few moments while we all digested Gialli's summary. Therefore, I was able to take in some of my astounding surroundings. The elegant Renaissance churches, the tranquil piazzas liberally decorated with magnificent fountains and the austere arches that commemorated the ancient imperial triumphs of this once-dominant city. Holmes's strident voice interrupted my reverie.

'Inspector Gialli, your very fine theories aside, are there any other facts that you can furnish us with, prior to our examination of the cardinal's office, which will aid us with our inquiry?' I was a little taken aback by the hostile edge to Holmes's voice and I could see that the good inspector was similarly hurt and surprised at Holmes's sharp questioning.

'There is little that I can add, save for my assurance that there is not one object nor speck of dust that has been moved nor disturbed since the moment of Cardinal Tosca's demise. Even the parchment remains where it fell, although its meaning is obscured by the ancient text in which it was written.' By the end of his reply a little zest had returned to Gialli's manner and as we turned into our hotel, which was situated conveniently and within easy access to all of Rome's major thoroughfares, Holmes congratulated him upon his efficiency.

The dapper little Italian bowed politely as he took his leave, assuring us that we should have access to Cardinal Tosca's office as soon as Pietro had made the necessary arrangements. Holmes was not particularly impressed with the dictates of Vatican etiquette, but realized that both he and Gialli were in the hands of the cardinals.

We soon discovered that our rooms were airy and quite spacious and once I had completed my unpacking I looked in on Holmes to see if he was going to join me for some dinner and a turn around the Roman Forum, which was barely a half mile away from our hotel. To my surprise Holmes agreed to both of my suggestions.

We took our meal at the hotel and it was notable for the many variations of pasta that it contained and a carafe of some rather pleasant Chianti. We sauntered along the Via Nazionale whilst we finished our cigars and passed the market and column of Trajan on our way to the Palatine Hill, which was at the heart of the Forum.

It was quite dark by the time that we had reached its base and we were forced to abandon any hopes that we might have had of exploring the corridors of the ancient palace. We decided to circumnavigate the exterior instead, but we were disappointed to note that the outlines of the buildings were shrouded.

Their austere magnificence now assumed the shape of dark and ominous mounds and the ghosts of the ancient past seemed to howl upon the winds that roamed along the blood-stained corridors of absolute power. I turned up my collar and suggested that we return to our hotel for a nightcap.

Holmes nodded his agreement emphatically.

'The seat of power may have shifted from the Palatine to the Vatican, Watson, but its hold over the populace has not lessened with the passing of the centuries,' Holmes observed, once we had begun to retrace our steps.

'Whatever do you mean, old fellow?' I asked.

'Ask yourself this, where else in the modern civilized world would the investigation into the murderous death of a prominent official be delayed by the observation of irrelevant ritual and etiquette?' I could think of no feasible reply, but became alarmed by Holmes's controversial observation.

'Have a care, Holmes. We must not ruffle too many feathers here or I fear that our investigation might well be over before it has even begun!' I warned quietly. Holmes merely grunted impatiently and quickened his stride towards our hotel.

CHAPTER FIVE

AT LAST ... A CLUE!

Before retiring we had arranged to be awoken for an early breakfast on the following morning. However, as soon as I arrived in the dining room, I could tell that my friend had been awake for a considerably longer time than I had been.

His rolls of ham and cheese had only been partially consumed and his empty coffee cup was already full of the ashes of at least two of his cigarettes. Holmes was amused by my observations and the look of disapproval upon my face.

'Well, Doctor, it is certainly most gracious of you to join your old friend for the first meal of the day!' Holmes cheerfully greeted me.

'Sometimes I wonder if you ever bother sleeping at all!' I responded.

'In common with my eating habits and requirements, I have discovered that sleep is only of benefit when it becomes absolutely necessary.' Graciously Holmes invited me to join him at the table with a wide sweep of his arm and as I settled into my chair he continued with his response.

'When one is blessed, or perhaps even cursed, with a mind as active and vital as mine, even the notion of sleep appears to be a complete waste of time. Watson, your ill-gotten knowledge of the sport of kings should surely have taught you by now that it is often a mistake to rein in a magnificent stallion. Undoubtedly, if you intend to win the race you must surely give him his head!'

I could not help but smile at my friend's total lack of humility. Yet, were I to think back to the many occasions when I had chastised him for taking liberties with his health, I was forced to admit that he did seem to thrive on the abstinence that he imposed upon himself once he was engaged upon a case. Perhaps Sherlock Holmes was not only able to resist and conquer the forces of evil that were constantly raised against him, but also the accepted laws of medical science!

As I tucked into a breakfast that was certainly no more than adequate, I glanced across at my friend and realized that the impending case supplied him with all of the sustenance that he required and his eyes were alive with the fire of adventure and excitement. Throughout the meal he remained in a quiet and meditative mood, yet I was certain that his unknown quarry would soon feel the full force of his fire.

As the day wore on, however, Holmes's contemplative mood gradually mutated into a restless and broody state of mind that finally became one of impatience and frustration. The reason for this deterioration was clear: the carriage to the Vatican, which Gialli had promised to him, had not yet arrived. Breakfast soon became lunchtime and Holmes retired to his room and his pipes.

From the other side of the door I could hear the echoes of him pacing endlessly around the cold marble floor of his room. I could almost see the contortions upon his anxious face and the endless plumes of smoke billowing from the bowl of his brier. I was becoming fretful myself and soon decided to maintain a vigil in a luxuriant white leather chair that was stationed close to the hotel's reception.

It would be mid afternoon before we were finally put out of our misery. We were met by the landau once again, although on this occasion the cheerful face of Inspector Gialli was not there to greet us. Nevertheless, I bounded up the stairs enthusiastically to alert Holmes and he joined me within an instant. Once again our carriage moved at a frustratingly sedate pace and we were accompanied by two of Gialli's uniformed officers.

Throughout the journey to the Vatican, Holmes sat in a pensive silence and I hoped that his pent-up frustration would not prohibit his diplomacy when dealing with our eminent employers. He remained oblivious to the architectural wonders that bounded our route through Rome and he only became vaguely interested as we neared our destination.

We crossed the River Tiber with the ancient ruins of the Mulvian Bridge sitting to our right and the austere, cylindrical edifice, known as the Castel Sant'Angelo, ahead of us. This interesting building was in an impressive state of repair considering its great age. The Emperor Hadrian had had it built in the early part of the second century AD as a family mausoleum and in subsequent centuries various popes had used it as a fortress and prison. It was comforting to recall that contemporary popes were of a more peaceful and benevolent nature!

The sheer thrill of passing through the unfeasible splendours of the Church of St Peter for the first time was impossible even for Sherlock Holmes to ignore and by the time that we had reached the entrance to the Vatican he was ready to leap from the carriage even before it had come to a halt. However, as it transpired, our frustration was to continue for a while longer yet.

The escort that Gialli had provided us with merely led us to the entrance of the venerated Sistine Chapel. There we were greeted by a small escort of the Swiss Guard who appeared to assume responsibility from Gialli's men once they had retreated to the landau.

The colourful regalia of the guard were startling enough in itself. Their jackets and medieval doubloons were decorated in broad vertical stripes of blue and gold, which were touched off with dashes of red. Upon their feet they wore unusual, soft flat shoes that resembled domestic slippers and upon their heads sat an angular metal helmet crowned with a plume of bright scarlet feathers. However, the fact that they were each bearing an eight-foot wooden pike made me feel most uneasy.

'In heaven's name, Holmes, anyone would think that it is you and I who are the criminals!' I whispered in a tone that would have been audible to Holmes alone.

Holmes greeted my assertion and our current situation with a surprisingly stoic silence and he did not display any of the indications of impatience and irritation that I might have expected from him. Perhaps our hallowed surroundings had stilled his restless soul, for his features were as composed and serene as I had ever seen them.

Our grasp of Italian was inadequate to the task of asking our gaudy escort as to the reason for our delay and detention and we took to the seats that had been indicated to us in the centre of the chapel. Inevitably our gaze was drawn to the remarkable and celebrated ceiling above our heads.

The scale and grandeur of this epic work of art made it impossible to believe that Michelangelo had been working under the most arduous conditions imaginable, over a period of four years! It was not enough that the pope, Julius II, was constantly berating him for the length of time that the ceiling was taking, but the process of painting directly onto plaster while constantly staring vertically above was almost impossible to conceive.

Holmes was following my awestruck gaze towards the wonders above us and even from this great distance we had no great difficulty in making out the vivid depictions of the various saints and biblical characters that decorated the large cornices. However, there was certainly no mistaking the renowned subject matter within the centre of the ceiling: the Almighty bestowing life upon the outstretched hand of Adam.

I passed on my observations to my friend, who was seated close by to me. Almost inevitably, however, his interpretation was vastly different to my own.

'You know, Watson, I find it most difficult to reconcile the sumptuous adornments and the glittering treasures that surround us with the humble origins of the man to whose name they have been dedicated. After all, was he not little more than the son of a simple carpenter? Did he not preach, on many occasions, upon the virtues of distributing one's fortune amongst those who are in the most need?' Holmes concluded by indicating the chapel's adornments with a dramatic sweep of his arm.

'Oh, come along, Holmes, even you, with your detached outlook, cannot possibly cast a harsh judgement upon these wonders!' I protested, with not a little surprise in my voice.

Holmes shook his head slowly with a wry smile.

'Watson, it appears that you still have much to learn about the ways of the world. Do you not realize that the basis of organized religion is nothing more than an endless list of laws and precepts, bound within the confines of a book? Surely, when that moment finally arrives, the ultimate judgement upon us will not be based upon the number of times that we have recited from that book, but more upon the manner in which we have behaved towards our fellow man.

'On more than one occasion you have been witness to and recorded for posterity my lack of discrimination between a duke or a king and a man of more humble means. It cannot merely be coincidence that more poverty seems to exist within those countries that view religious doctrine as a form of sacrificial diligence, than those that adopt a more humble service.'

At that moment Holmes paused while he rummaged in his pockets for a cigarette. I gestured towards our surroundings and as there was still no indication that we were to be greeted by our client, I suggested that we smoke outside.

I found it very difficult to counter my friend's controversial hypothesis. At once my mind went back to our interview with the King of Bohemia[1], at the outset of the Irene Adler affair, and then to Holmes's treatment of the ultimately tragic Randell Crosby[2] and the kindness that he had bestowed upon him. Save for the waiving of fees, in the case of Crosby, Holmes had viewed them both as clients and nothing more or less.

I was on the point of continuing with our irreverent discourse when the somewhat ashen face of Inspector Gialli appeared at the chapel door. In the shadows behind him stood a particularly tall figure whose height was exaggerated by his slight build, long flowing robe and the high skull cap upon his balding head. As we approached the chapel door, the tall figure came out to greet us and I could tell from the red cap and robe that this was none other than our client, Cardinal Pietro.

He held out his long, sinewy fingers in order that we might place a kiss upon his ring, in the time-honoured tradition, while Gialli made the formal introductions.

'Excuse me, signori, but Cardinal Pietro apologizes for his poor English and has requested that I act as his interpreter, with your kind permission, of course,' Gialli asked humbly.

Holmes and I nodded our heads in assent and Pietro invited us back into the chapel.

'The cardinal wishes me to thank you for having made so long and strenuous journey on his behest. He also repeats his request for absolute discretion throughout and especially at the close of your investigation,' Gialli continued while we made our way through the chapel and onward through an absolute labyrinth of oak panel-lined corridors.

Again we nodded.

Finally we arrived at the door to an office that was easily identified as that of Cardinal Tosca by members of the Swiss Guard on duty on either side of the door. At this point, the cardinal leaned down and whispered earnestly into Gialli's ear. Gialli cleared his throat and appeared to be somewhat embarrassed before he made the cardinal's intentions known to us. He spoke with uncertainty in his voice and with frequent pauses.

'Mr Holmes, it appears that the cardinal did not realize that it was your intention to travel with Doctor Watson and that as a consequence of the delicate nature of the case, he insists that the doctor remains out here while you conduct your investigation in the office.' As if in anticipation of Holmes's reaction to this request, Gialli was almost breathless by the time that he had completed his sentence.

I was on the point of turning on my heels when Holmes rounded angrily upon the hapless detective.

'No, Inspector Gialli, this will not do! It is not sufficient that my colleague and I have been kept waiting for nigh on twenty-four hours, but now you expect us to suffer this fresh insult? Kindly ask the cardinal to reimburse us for the cost of a return ticket to London while we make our travel plans for an immediate departure!'

I was not certain if it was I or Gialli who was the most dismayed at Holmes's violent although not altogether surprising reaction. Nevertheless, in an instant Holmes began to retrace his steps and I followed in his slipstream, while reflecting upon the use that the Castel Sant'Angelo had been put to in a bygone age!

I found my friend pacing back and forth outside, in a state of great agitation, while almost chewing his way through a cigarette.

'We shall have to walk back to our hotel if the carriage doesn't return for us at once!' he snapped angrily.

I was mortified and speechless, secure in the knowledge that nobody, save for Sherlock Holmes, had ever spoken to a Vatican cardinal in such a fashion. I waited by my friend's side while he attempted to regain his composure.

'Watson, I am afraid that I might have seriously jeopardized our further involvement in a case that promised to be one of our most intriguing and challenging to date!' Holmes glanced apologetically towards me for his anger had now subsided into deep regret.

'Do not judge yourself too harshly, old friend. You had demonstrated great patience up to this moment and their treatment of you has been decidedly shoddy, to say the least. I do appreciate the stand that you made on my behalf.'

Holmes smiled half-heartedly at my attempts at consolation and stared reflectively towards the entrance to the Sistine Chapel.

We stood in like fashion for what seemed to be an eternity when, to our great relief, we saw Gialli walk tentatively towards us.

'Signori, the cardinal deeply regrets any distress that he may have caused you and hopes that you might reconsider and return to Cardinal Tosca's office to solve the mystery of his untimely death!' Gialli interpreted by way of a proclamation. Then he dropped his voice as he continued, 'To tell you the truth, Mr Holmes, I sincerely hope that you might reconsider as well. This case is clearly beyond my abilities.'

Not surprisingly, this last statement of the inspector surely had the desired effect. Holmes put his arm around Gialli's shoulders and said encouragingly, 'Oh, come along, Inspector, it is as much an assault upon the truth to denigrate one's own abilities as it is to overstate them. We shall embark upon this case in tandem!' Holmes called this last statement over his shoulder as he strode purposefully back towards the chapel, while Gialli and I followed.

This time, as we approached Cardinal Tosca's office, the Swiss Guardsmen immediately stood aside and Pietro invited us to enter with a bow and a wave of his arm. As soon as he had entered the room, Holmes was transformed and he became oblivious to his surroundings and his audience. His eyes seemed to take in every detail with a startling rapidity and he motioned to us all that no one else should enter the room while he conducted his initial examination.

It was most gratifying for me to observe the looks of awe and admiration upon the faces of Cardinal Pietro and Inspector Gialli as my friend went about his work. One moment he was scrabbling around upon the floor with his magnifying glass in hand, while the next he was examining the window sill in the most minute detail.

It was at this point that a moment of startling realization seemed to come upon him and he ceased from his frantic movements while emitting a low subdued whistle. Not wishing to disturb any potential clues that lay upon the desk, Holmes sank down upon the floor and sat on his haunches. He turned his attention towards Gialli, seemingly unaware of the raised eyebrows that his unusual situation had provoked.

'Inspector Gialli, please explain to me, with absolute accuracy, the events and the exact circumstances that led to the untimely demise of Cardinal Tosca.' Holmes closed his eyes and pursed his lips with a raised forefinger.

Somewhat nervously, Gialli rummaged in his inside pocket for his notebook.

'From the account of the cardinal's personal assistant,

Father Roberto Bettega, it appears that of late the cardinal had been spending an unusual length of time locked away alone within his office. This change of routine seems to have coincided with the arrival upon his desk of a large number of unusual scrolls of ancient papyrus—'

Holmes halted the inspector with an urgently raised arm and a suppressed laugh of surprising pleasure.

'Ancient papyrus, you say. That is a rather unusual description, would you not say, Inspector?'

'That is exactly what I thought, Signor Holmes, but I assure you that I am merely quoting from Father Bettega's statement. Apparently the scrolls were delivered to the cardinal personally by way of a special courier who had arrived unexpectedly from Egypt.'

'This would have been how long ago?' Holmes indicated that I should be making good use of my own notebook by this time and rather impatiently invited me to join him in the room.

'Exactly three days before the cardinal's death. Since that time the cardinal had been working tirelessly at his desk, both day and night, in an effort at translating the scroll from its ancient Aramaic script. He regarded it as a task of the utmost importance and urgency and it was work that demanded total vigilance on his part. Consequently no one was allowed to enter this room when he was translating the scroll.'

'Not even Father Bettega, or Cardinal Pietro here?' Holmes asked while closely observing the cardinal for his reaction to Gialli's reply. In this Holmes was not entirely without success, for Pietro ground his teeth and turned away rather petulantly.

Gialli shook his head gravely.

'No, Signor Holmes, Cardinal Tosca would only allow access to one member of the Swiss Guard on those rare occasions when he permitted himself some food. At all other times the scroll would need to be secure within his safe before

Tosca would grant admission to another soul.'

'Yet it appears that someone else did gain access to the room while the scroll was out of the safe,' Holmes said quietly and almost to himself.

'Who might that have been, Signor Holmes?' Cardinal Pietro asked from the doorway, by way of Gialli's translation

'Why, the murderer, of course,' Holmes replied with a cursory smile.

'But Holmes, the murderer would hardly have been invited into the office by Cardinal Tosca himself!' I protested. 'Besides, did the inspector not inform us earlier that the murderer had gained access to the room by way of forcing the window? You were certainly examining the blade marks upon it for long enough.'

'Quite so, Watson, quite so …' Holmes's voice tailed away for a moment while he seemed to gather his thoughts. Then he leapt back to his feet in a single fluid movement that clearly alarmed the cardinal with its abruptness. He invited Gialli to continue reading from his notes with a crook of his finger.

'How was the alarm first raised and by whom?' Holmes asked impatiently while the inspector rummaged through his book.

'Father Bettega was now used to the cardinal's irregular hours, so when he discovered that he was still hard at work, even at such an unseemly hour, Bettega decided to retire for the night, in dismay but with little surprise.

'On the following morning, however, when Bettega arrived at the cardinal's room with his breakfast, he found the room empty and the bed not slept in! At once he raced down to the office and when his constant beating upon the door produced no response, he summoned the Swiss Guard to force their way in.' Gialli indicated the broken lock to Holmes, who examined it briefly with his glass. It must have been a surprisingly weak lock for the efforts of the guards had produced very little structural damage to the door and its frame.

'This is all very well, Inspector, but where is the key?' Holmes asked in a state of some exasperation.

The colour drained from the face of the hard-pressed inspector, once he had realized his uncharacteristic omission.

'I do not know, Signor Holmes.' Gialli shook his head disconsolately.

'Was it not discovered when the body of the cardinal was examined, nor when you had the room searched?' Holmes persisted.

Again Gialli shook his head.

'I do not understand – there simply must have been a key!' I exclaimed. I was as confused by the absence of the key as I was by Holmes's calm and almost gratified reaction to this fact.

'Mark that well, Watson, for unless I am very much mistaken, it may well prove to be a fact of the utmost significance,' Holmes instructed.

At this juncture Cardinal Pietro whispered in Gialli's ear a few agitated words of Italian. To everyone's surprise, Holmes responded with no apparent need of interpretation.

'No, Cardinal, my outlandish methods have not brought us any closer to the solving of the mystery, just yet. There is still much work to be done and I am not a miracle worker! Do not look so surprised, Watson, you forget that Latin lies at the root of the Italian tongue and I had my head filled with that ancient tongue from a very early age.' Holmes smiled when he noticed Pietro's obvious discomfort, but instead turned his attention towards Inspector Gialli.

'Now, Inspector, to the desk. Kindly indicate to me, if you would, the exact location of Cardinal Tosca's head when he was discovered by the Swiss Guard.'

Despite Holmes's smile of encouragement, Gialli was most hesitant when he entered the room. He moved to a position behind the desk and once he was satisfied that Holmes had completed his examination, Gialli sat upon the wooden swivel chair and with a pencil drew a rough outline of a head that lay adjacent to a large, dry bloodstain.

Once he had completed his task Holmes joined him behind the desk and examined Gialli's crude artwork.

'You are absolutely certain as to the position of Tosca's head?' Holmes queried.

Gialli nodded his head emphatically.

'As you can see, Signor Holmes, the parchment that the cardinal was working on is inexplicably distant from where the tragedy occurred, hence my assertion that the murderer had been interrupted in his task,' Gialli repeated.

'Yet he appeared to have had enough time to lock the door and take the key away with him,' Holmes said quietly, almost under his breath. 'Oh but, Inspector, there are many papers missing from this desk!'

Once again Gialli appeared to be greatly perplexed.

'I assured you earlier, Signor Holmes, that nothing had been removed from this room prior to your arrival. How can you possibly make such a statement with any certainty, when the parchment is still sitting here upon the desk?'

Holmes picked up a cardboard tube, wrapped in brown paper, which had hitherto been sitting unnoticed on the edge of the desk. He examined the open end of the tube with his glass before bringing it to Gialli's close attention.

'See here, Inspector, how each twist of the tube has begun to gape under the pressure of its bulging contents. Again here, observe how strained the string that secured the wrapping paper has become.' Holmes picked up the remaining pile of parchment and dropped it disdainfully back upon the desk top.

'Do you honestly believe that these few sheets would have caused such an effect upon the tube?'

Gialli shook his head once again.

'I do not know how I should have overlooked this, and what has become of the missing parchments?'

'That remains to be seen, Inspector, however if you were to get the remaining sheets translated and bring them to our hotel, I should be able to enlighten you further. I assume that the relevant parties have all been interviewed and that none of them speak a word of English?'

'You are correct, Signor Holmes.'

'Can I also assume that the body of Cardinal Tosca has been cleaned, dressed and made ready for his funeral?'

Again Gialli nodded his confirmation.

'Therefore any examination by Doctor Watson would be a complete and utter waste of time! Watson, I believe that we have concluded our business here. Inspector, perhaps you would also bring the transcripts of your interviews with you when you drop by with the translation.'

Before the inspector had a chance to respond to this latest request, Holmes was bustling his way through the office door and with barely a cursory acknowledgement to Cardinal Pietro, he was gone. I smiled apologetically before following closely behind him.

CHAPTER SIX

AN AUDIENCE

GIALLI WAITED WITH us until the landau had returned and we used that time in making our arrangements for the delivery of the translated scrolls. We were on the point of boarding that stately carriage when a Swiss Guardsman ran urgently and somewhat awkwardly towards us. He spoke breathlessly to the inspector while his awestruck eyes remained firmly fixed upon my friend.

'Signor Holmes, it seems that His Holiness the Pope wishes to grant you a private audience!' Gialli announced with a hushed, reverent excitement that was entirely understandable under the circumstances.

Without a glimmer of emotion, Holmes stepped down from the landau once more.

'I do not recall asking for an audience,' Holmes mentioned quietly while the guardsman led him back towards the Vatican. We all believed that it would be more appropriate if Gialli and I waited by the carriage and we both smoked in an anxious silence.

Once or twice we touched upon the subject of Holmes's examination of Tosca's office and we agreed that it was a pointless exercise to speculate upon my friend's conclusions. However, Gialli did mention the fact that Tosca had always been seen as the Pope's natural successor and that his recent erratic behaviour was potentially throwing this assumed succession into some doubt.

Holmes had been gone for little more than half an hour and upon his return he could not be persuaded to discuss his audience in any detail. He merely described Pope Leo XIII as a white-haired gentleman of a kindly disposition who spoke to Holmes in soft modulated tones by way of his personal interpreter. It was only once Gialli had returned to conclude his business in Tosca's office and our landau had begun its return journey to our hotel that Holmes spoke in a little more detail about the rare privilege that he had been granted

'Watson, I can only apologize to both you and your beleaguered readers for my reticence in revealing further details of my meeting with the Pope, but protocol dictates that I do not. However, if you are to take an intelligent interest in proceedings I should mention one or two of the more relevant aspects of our conversation. Notwithstanding this, I must call upon you to employ the same level of diplomacy as I have just been sworn to,' Holmes insisted.

'You can always rely upon my discretion, Holmes,' I confirmed.

'I had no doubt, Watson! Very well then, although the majority of our interview was somewhat dry and of little consequence, His Holiness did raise one point of intrigue, although as to its significance I cannot, as yet, decide. As you might imagine he repeated his request for a rapid and discreet conclusion to the case. However, his whole demeanour altered when I broached the subject of the scrolls.

'I could tell, even without the aid of the interpreter, who was singularly unemployed while His Holiness stood up slowly to consider his response, that the subject of the scrolls was one with which he was not entirely comfortable. I must confess that his reply, when it finally came, was not one that I had by any means expected.'

I could not help but smile at my friend's furrowed brow and his troubled expression as he considered the very notion of his having been surprised. Though I must admit that such an occurrence was indeed a rarity, I was appalled at the conceit that would not broker such an awful accident! At that moment Holmes remembered the presence of our police escort and he motioned me to silence with a finger raised to his lips.

Despite my burning curiosity, we completed what remained of the journey without exchanging a solitary word. As I smoked my pipe, my mind went over everything that we had just seen and heard and it was only once we had reached our hotel that I realized that I had been oblivious to the sights of Rome that had so enthralled me on our outward journey.

We had arrived at our hotel just as dinner was being served, but Holmes merely sat with me, over a cup of coffee, while I ate. I noticed that he was smiling somewhat patronizingly at my efforts to negate my hunger in as short a time as possible. No doubt he was aware that I wished him to continue with his account of his audience with the Pope, but I had to wait until the meal was over and we found ourselves sauntering along the Via Nazionale once more before he broached the subject

When he did so it was with much reluctance and I was also appalled to note the extreme lengths that he went to in assuring that we were not to be overheard. The thoroughfare was almost deserted and yet Holmes glanced furtively, this way and that, time and again before he was satisfied that there was nobody within earshot.

'In heaven's name, Holmes, what is the meaning behind all of this skulduggery?' I exclaimed with some exasperation.

'I assure you, Watson, that we cannot afford to be too cautious,' Holmes replied in a tone that was barely louder than a whisper. 'As I anticipated we are currently dealing with forces far beyond any of our previous experience. Before I can formulate a cohesive theory, however, it is absolutely essential that we receive the translated scrolls from Gialli.'

'I cannot, for the life of me, understand the importance that you attach to a pile of ancient scrolls.'

'Nor should I, Watson, were it not for the manner of His Holiness's reaction to my raising of the subject. As I earlier described, he stood up slowly and spent some time in formulating his thoughtful reply. He informed me, carefully but emphatically, that there are only four Gospels.'

'Well, of course there are!' I declared in a state of astonishment. 'Surely such a statement was superfluous?'

'You would think so, Watson, especially as I had made no mention of the Gospels, much less the fact that there might be more than four of them. Yet there was also the merest trace of a threat in the manner of his statement and I was left in little doubt that any further discussion of the scrolls would be displeasing to him.'

'So the question we need to ask ourselves is why the Pope should be so disturbed by the existence of the scrolls. I see now why you are so keen to see the translation.' Then a further thought occurred to me. 'Surely you are not suggesting that His Holiness is implicated in Tosca's death in any way?'

Holmes's continued silence was as shocking to me as the most outrageous answer that he might have mustered.

'After all, the shape of the weapon used seems to direct us towards our violent visitor at Baker Street,' I suggested. Again my friend remained silent until I pointed out that one of the symbols that the Bedouin had worn about his belt had also been present at the base of one of the parchments.

Holmes stared at me as if my last statement had struck a violent chord, then he shook his head.

'Watson, this case is not yet clear to me. The facts, as far as we can understand them, seem to point the finger of guilt squarely towards the Bedouin. Apart from the nature of the weapon used, we also know that the scrolls came from Egypt, which is surely the birthplace of our expansive friend. Furthermore, we also know that he is a follower of the Coptic Church, which boasts the oldest place of Christian worship that we know of....' Holmes paused for a further protracted silence and I could not refrain from interjecting.

'What better motive for the death of Cardinal Tosca could there be than to reclaim a sacred parchment on behalf of the oldest church on earth?' I asked excitedly.

Apparently my friend was still some way from being convinced by my argument and we returned to our hotel in a contemplative silence.

CHAPTER SEVEN

A WIRE TO MRS HUDSON

I COULD NOT understand why Holmes was so reluctant to even consider the validity of my argument. I even began to wonder if a mind as evolved as his would sometimes seek a more obtuse solution to a problem when a simpler and less challenging explanation was under his nose all along.

Yet he was, above all, a man of logic and I was certain that he would never shy away from the truth merely for the sake of extending his powers to their limits. Nevertheless, I took him to task over his continued reluctance to discuss the Bedouin theory once we had returned to the hotel.

We took our cognacs up to Holmes's room and it was there that I raised the long-forgotten subject of the wires that he had despatched from Baker Street to his colleagues: Berlajous and Elraji.

'I presume that you sent these messages as a means of tracing the movements of the Bedouin prior to his arrival at Baker Street?' I suggested once we had settled down with our drinks.

'You presume correctly, friend Watson, although I must immediately point out that neither have so far offered me a reply. The Bedouin's point of origin and his current location are as much a mystery now as they were at the time of our first encounter,' Holmes replied.

'That is, apart from the very tangible fact that the weapon which he favours has, apparently, been used in perpetrating a most heinous crime, right here in the city of Rome!' I exclaimed.

'Apparently, Watson, apparently, but we must not be too hasty in reaching premature conclusions. I shall do nothing more until I have read the translation of the scrolls. Do not forget, Watson, the Church of St Mark was founded in AD 41 and it is, therefore, the oldest known church in the world. It is completely understandable that the Holy See would have a vested interest in an ancient scroll that originates from that source. Our investigation can only move forward once we fully understand its nature.'

I shook my head in disbelief.

'I never cease to be amazed at the detailed knowledge that you possess on such a vast array of different subjects. Now I am well able to understand your keen interest in the parchment,' I concluded.

I looked up suddenly and became aware that my friend had been oblivious to my last statement. From under his breath I heard him repeat the warning we had received from the Bedouin in our rooms and as he lit his pipe I could see his eyes drift away as his thoughts began to sink into the furthest recesses of his remarkable mind.

For my part, I was deathly tired and so decided to retire to my room for the night.

The following morning I was not especially surprised to discover that Holmes had spent the entire night in his chair and at his pipes. However, despite his night of abuse, I was amazed to see just how fresh and alert he seemed, and that before breakfast he had already despatched a wire to Mrs

Hudson. Holmes steadfastly refused to divulge its contents and by the time we had concluded our breakfast I was resigned to it remaining a mystery for the foreseeable future.

Once again Holmes and I spent yet another fruitless morning as we awaited the arrival of the normally reliable Inspector Gialli, together with the potential means of shedding some light upon our current mystery. By noon Holmes was positively wrought with impatience and frustration as neither the manuscript nor the reply from London presented themselves.

When a visitor did finally turn up, we were disappointed to note that he had arrived empty-handed and that he was not Inspector Gialli!

Inspector De Rossi was only a subordinate of Gialli and it appeared that his main qualification, for the mission to our hotel, was that he possessed a mastery of the English language that was by no means inferior to that of his principal. De Rossi had no knowledge of the case whatsoever, but it had fallen upon him to impart some shocking news to us.

Apparently Gialli had been successful in having the parchment translated for us. However, shortly after he had left for our hotel he had been set upon by a pair of ruffians who then beat him to within an inch of his life!

'Good heavens!' I exclaimed. Then, once I had fully digested this awful news, I asked, 'Surely there must have been some of his officers in attendance, especially as he was upon such a vital mission?'

'Sadly, no, Signor, the translator lives within a short walk of the Via Nazionale, so the inspector decided to dispense with the use of an escort and present the document to you on his own.

'The package was quite innocuous in its appearance so there was no reason for him to have been wary of an attack. Who would have suspected that he was carrying anything of such importance? The inspector was very popular with all who worked with him,' De Rossi added sadly.

In contrast, my friend appeared to have been more concerned about the whereabouts of the translation than he was about Gialli himself.

'I take it that the package has disappeared as thoroughly as have the ruffians?' Holmes asked resignedly.

'Indeed it has, Signor Holmes, there is no trace of either the package or the perpetrators of this evil deed.'

I was aghast to see that Holmes seemed to be mildly amused by De Rossi's dramatic and emotional statement, though surely not by the fate of our beleaguered colleague?

'Were there any witnesses who are able to describe Gialli's assailants?'

'The translator lives in a very small side turning that runs parallel to the Via Nazionale, so there were very few people around save for an elderly street vendor. However, he does seem to be in possession of most of his faculties and he described the assailants as large, thick-set gentlemen dressed smartly in dark brown suits and soft flat caps.

'The remarkable thing is, Signor Holmes, that during the commotion voices became raised, as you might expect, and the vendor is adamant that they both spoke in refined English accents.'

'That does not make any sense at all!' I exclaimed. 'After all, the only person who would have known about the importance of Gialli's package would have been the murderer himself and ...'

Holmes hushed me with a rapid hand movement and then began to usher De Rossi from the room before I could utter another word.

'Thank you, Inspector De Rossi, for your excellent report. I trust that you will be kind enough to let us know the minute that Gialli is well enough to be questioned.'

'Sadly that moment might be some time in arriving.' De Rossi shook his head forlornly. 'The inspector's injuries are most severe,' he added as he closed the door slowly behind him.

'Well, I must say, Holmes, you appeared to be more concerned about the fate of the missing papers than you were about the condition of a colleague!' I protested.

'Watson, Inspector Gialli will undoubtedly recover his health in due course, whereas the missing scrolls might well be lost forever. Although their value has yet to be established, they are already responsible for a man's life and another is now hanging in the balance. This entire case appears to rotate around the papers that Tosca died for.'

'I can see that now, but I do not understand why you ushered De Rossi from the room while I was trying to establish a point of significance. After all, he is a policeman!' I persisted.

'Remember, Watson, it is only we two who have any knowledge of the Bedouin and his intervention. The significance of the shape of the murder weapon will mean nothing to the Roman police force and I did not wish you to say anything that might divert them from their own line of inquiry. Besides, De Rossi appeared to have no knowledge of the case and it might not be prudent for us to enlighten him if Gialli saw fit to maintain his ignorance,' Holmes explained.

'Surely you are not implying that De Rossi is not to be trusted?' I asked incredulously.

'At this moment I cannot be sure of anything. We must hope that Gialli will be fit enough to discuss things at the earliest possible moment. In the meantime we can do nothing more than wait,' Holmes concluded dejectedly.

We sat in silence for a moment or two with our pipes.

'Holmes, why should two well-dressed Englishmen attack an Italian policeman and then make off with a package, the contents of which they could not possibly have had any prior knowledge? After all, only the murderer and perhaps Father Bettega had any notion that the scrolls were of value. We have forged a link between the Bedouin and the scrolls, and his weapon of choice, or its like, was certainly the cause of Tosca's death. Yet these Englishmen have attached as much importance to the scrolls that were left behind as you appear to,' I concluded in a state of some despair.

Holmes turned towards me with a dismissive grunt.

'Watson, do you not see that the value of the scrolls, which were left behind on Tosca's desk, is only implied?' he asked cantankerously.

'I am sorry, I simply do not understand. Inspector Gialli clearly stated that the only reason that some of the scrolls were left behind was because the murderer had been interrupted suddenly. He would not have had time to discriminate between the various scrolls,' I insisted.

'That was merely speculation on his part and speculation is a soft and precarious foundation on which to build any case, much less one as complex and obtuse as this one is. Once again, Watson, you are forgetting about the key.'

'Are you saying that you no longer hold to the theory that the Bedouin is the culprit?'

'On the contrary, I think it most likely that he is. However, I will not commit myself further until I receive more data. We must hope that Inspector Gialli makes a speedy recovery.' There was something dismissive in the manner in which Holmes turned away from me this time and I left him quietly to his thoughts.

The two items of news, which we had been waiting most anxiously for, arrived within a few minutes of each other. It has to be said that neither of them imbued us with too much hope.

The bulletin from the hospital was a double-edged sword.

Obviously we were delighted to hear that the life of the genial Roman policeman was now no longer in danger. However, the doctors also informed us that he would be in no condition to be interviewed by us, or by anybody else, for that matter, for several days yet. Holmes proceeded to wring his hands in frustration once we were informed of the latter and he hurled the offending piece of paper to the floor, in disgust.

Nevertheless, it was the wire from Mrs Hudson that seemed to cause him the most anxiety. She confirmed that there had been no replies to the wires Holmes had despatched to both Berlajous and Elraji. As frustrating to hear as this was, it was as nothing when compared to the disturbing information that we had received from our old friend Dave 'Gunner' King.

King had managed to trace the very colleague of his who had deposited the Bedouin at our door on that most fateful morning. Not only had the Bedouin not arrived in London by way of the boat train, as Holmes had originally but erroneously asserted, but there had been no further information that would suggest that he had subsequently departed!

'So the blackguard still remains in London,' I asserted.

'So it would appear, Watson,' Holmes responded quietly.

Holmes moved over to the window and gazed mournfully towards the teeming and colourful thoroughfare that wound its way towards the ancient Roman forum. He pressed a forefinger against his lips and he only broke his silence once his plans were in place. Evidently he had come to a most startling conclusion.

'Watson, we must make our departure from Rome as promptly as the necessary arrangements will allow!'

'I cannot believe that you intend to retreat from the battlefield before a victory has been won,' I responded in disbelief.

'Surely the implications of our correspondence are clear? Inspector Gialli's indisposition renders it impossible for us to ascertain the true nature of his attack, much less the exact meaning of the scrolls.

'Moreover, the fact that our Bedouin friend still remains in London seems to shift the theatre of conflict in a more westerly direction. The vendor's evidence that Gialli's assailants spoke with cultured English accents does not seem so fanciful now, eh, Watson?' Holmes suggested with some excitement.

I lit a cigarette and smoked thoughtfully for a moment or two while I digested the meaning behind this new information.

'Are you suggesting that the Bedouin is, in some way, connected to the Englishmen that attacked Gialli?'

'It is too early to make that assertion, Watson. However, the Bedouin is certainly leaving himself exposed and vulnerable while he remains in London and I very much doubt that he would take such a risk without good reason.'

'Yes, but I cannot even begin to imagine what that reason might be,' I admitted.

'That is precisely why I propose that you return to London with all speed! I am certain that with your usual mixture of guile and tenacity you will soon provide me with the answers that I so sorely need.' I searched Holmes's eyes for a glint of humour, but I could find none.

'If you sincerely believe that I could be of greater use there, then of course I shall start to put my travel plans together immediately. I presume that you intend to remain here in Rome until your investigation into Cardinal Tosca's death is complete. No doubt Inspector Gialli will be of some assistance once he has fully recovered,' I suggested.

Holmes responded by poignantly shaking his head slowly back and forth. He was obviously wary of my reaction to what he next intended to propose, because he lit his pipe somewhat deliberately and seemed to go out of his way to avoid my gaze.

'Watson, I cannot afford the time it might take for Gialli to become of some use once again. I must take my own initiative and move my investigation to its point of origin: namely "the cradle of civilization", Egypt itself!' Holmes tentatively declared.

'I will not allow you to travel to such a land unattended!' I immediately protested. 'Nor shall I return to London until I have your assurance that you will not make such an undertaking until my return. It is not easy for me to forget the effect of your ruse at the Reichenbach Falls,[1] nor the potential danger that you exposed yourself to as a result of my enforced absence. I will not make that same mistake twice,' I pronounced to him emphatically.

Holmes appeared to be greatly perplexed by my reaction.

'Watson, I assure you that I would not have made such a proposal unless I felt it to be absolutely necessary. Nothing will be accomplished if I were to remain here or return with you to London. If we separate we can achieve much. I will rely on you to locate the Bedouin and then to ascertain the full extent of his involvement in this matter.

'Furthermore, I can think of no one better suited than my Watson for the task of ensuring that no harm befalls our cherished landlady, Mrs Hudson.' By now Holmes had resorted to the use of flattery as a force of persuasion; however, I was not to be so easily convinced.

'Do you really believe that Mrs Hudson's life might be in danger?'

Holmes responded by nodding his head slowly and with some gravity.

'Surely this time you go too far, Holmes. It is inconceivable that anyone should wish her to come to harm and I can certainly see no earthly reason for anyone willing to carry out such a heinous act.' Despite my scepticism it was impossible for me to conceal the anxiety from my voice.

'While the Bedouin remains in London there will always remain that possibility. Besides which, we have chosen to ignore his most emphatic and forceful warning, so the notion of him returning to 221b is surely not a fanciful one. Remember his parting words Watson, "This time it is only the chair." He is certainly not an individual to whose mercies I would entrust someone as vulnerable as Mrs Hudson!' Holmes dramatically concluded.

'Now I understand and of course I shall go. However, I should be less concerned about returning to London were I to be assured that you would delay your journey to Egypt until the time of my return,' I suggested, although I knew that there was little chance of my words being heeded.

'Have no fear, Watson. I am sure that you will recall how for three years, under my guise as Sigerson,[2] the Norwegian explorer of renown, I managed to traverse many regions far more treacherous and containing more dangers than any that I might encounter in Egypt. Despite the absence of the watchful eye of my most stalwart ally, you can be assured that I did manage to survive ... hah!' Holmes emphasized his point with a dramatic wave of his arms and I bowed my head in reluctant submission.

'You leave me with very little choice but pray tell me of your intentions once you arrive in Egypt. After all, you will be undertaking a very considerable journey.'

'In the absence of the scrolls and the incapacitated inspector, I have little choice but to continue my research in the land that spawned the scrolls in the first place. Where else might it be possible for me to gain a comprehension of their meaning?

'It goes without saying that, once I have gained an insight into their secrets, I should be able to gauge the motives behind both their theft and the murder of Cardinal Tosca, without my having to return to Rome. We have both observed the symbol of the Copts[3] upon the scrolls and upon the Bedouin's attire and Egypt abounds with some of the oldest churches within the Christian world. I must journey to Egypt!' Holmes confirmed with a determined emphasis.

Holmes must have observed a look of crestfallen defeat upon my face because he soon added, 'Naturally any information that you might gather in London, as to the movements and motives of our Bedouin friend, will doubtless prove to be of enormous value to me.'

I was certain that Holmes could sense the futility of trying to console me; nevertheless we began to make our travel arrangements without a moment's delay.

PART TWO

THE COPTIC PATRIARCHS

CHAPTER EIGHT

THE CRADLE OF CIVILIZATION

A T THIS JUNCTURE I feel duty bound to make an awful confession.

Anyone who has ever taken an intelligent interest in the chronicles that I have compiled of the cases and abilities of my friend Sherlock Holmes will be aware that I normally received my instructions from Holmes with a deference that was almost bordering on submission.

Such was the high esteem in which I held my friend that the very notion of my raising a query to his proposals, no matter how absurd they might have seemed to me at the time, was impossible for me to conceive. If an occasion did arise when I could no longer hold my tongue, it was usually to admonish Holmes for his flagrant abuse of himself in the pursuit of his quest for justice.

The very idea of my refusing to carry out an instruction of his had always been unthinkable to me, but an attempt by me to actually deceive the world's only consulting detective was surely bordering on insanity! Yet, as I went about the business of making the necessary travel arrangements, to Cairo for Holmes and to London for myself, an idea that would absolve me of all guilt in any eventuality began to germinate in my head.

I realized at once that if I was to put my plan into motion I would need to act with all speed and not a little cunning.

Holmes had left all of the preparations in my hands, as he had done on so many occasions in the past. Obviously this had given me the freedom to act in any way that I saw fit, although the need for discretion was paramount to the success of my deception. My first priority was to despatch two wires to London.

The first of these, to Mrs Hudson, was the more straightforward of the two. I advised her to ensure the security of 221b at all times and under every circumstance. She was to remain indoors for as long as this remained practical and she should enlist the aid of Billy, our occasional page boy, in carrying out all but the most essential of errands. I did not wish to alarm her unduly so I did not dwell upon the subject of the threatening Bedouin, but I left her in little doubt that my words of warning were not to be taken lightly.

I felt apprehensive barely a moment after the wire had been despatched. After all, had not Holmes insisted that my primary function in London was to have been to ensure the safety of our landlady? Why had the Bedouin remained in London?

We had been left in little doubt that Holmes had been kept under surveillance prior to the Bedouin's untimely intervention, so doubtless he and his confederates must have been aware of the fact that Holmes and I were no longer ensconced in Baker Street. So what were his motives in remaining? I quelled the rages of my conscience by reasoning that they would be something other than to bring harm upon Mrs Hudson.

To ease the heavy burden of my guilt still further, I decided to send a further wire. I had only ever encountered

Holmes's brother, Mycroft, on but three separate occasions[1] and each of these had led Holmes and I upon some of our most challenging adventures to date. Although both Holmes and Mycroft had been most reticent in discussing Mycroft's actual role within the British Government, I had been left in little doubt that it was a position that provided him with considerable resources and not a little influence. Who better to alert to the potential plight of Mrs Hudson and to provide a potent, watchful eye than he?

Within the wire I provided Mycroft with a brief albeit informative sketch of all that had transpired so far. I could see nothing detrimental in his possessing this information and I was convinced that the enormity of his brother's case would convince him of the need for action. I emphasize this point in view of Mycroft's not unjust reputation for a tendency towards lethargy.

Mycroft's entire existence revolved around a small triangular path that traversed the route between his lodgings, his office in Whitehall and his club of choice, the Diogenes. I decided that the surest way of my wire finding him would be to despatch it to his club and this followed the wire to Baker Street within minutes. I rubbed my hands together in satisfaction, so convinced was I that my absence from London would now prove to be of little consequence.

I informed both recipients that I would inform them of a return address as soon as I could establish one in Egypt. In the meantime I decided to delay our departure from Rome for as long as it would take for them to acknowledge receipt of my wires. To ensure this I contrived a story that there were no trains leaving for Brindisi within the next forty-eight hours.

Not surprisingly Holmes was irritated by the news, but he accepted my offer to remain with him in Rome until his time of departure. After all, there was still a slim chance that Gialli might make a sudden recovery and such a miracle would surely render both of our journeys as somewhat superfluous. That hope served to calm his nerves temporarily although he asked me to find out if an alternative route existed. Obviously I provided him with a further negative response, although I also realized that he would not be put off indefinitely.

The following two days were spent in a similar fashion. Repeated inquiries at the hospital, which yielded no further improvement in Gialli's condition, were followed by similarly ill-fated journeys to the station. Finally, when I began to realize that any further delays might contrive to jeopardize my entire plot, it was with some relief that I received my replies from London.

Mrs Hudson expressed her gratitude for my concern and assured me that she would follow my instructions to the letter. Although she added that she considered it to be 'a lot of fuss over nothing'!

On the other hand, Mycroft's reply turned out to be an entirely different kettle of fish altogether.

'My dear Doctor Watson, you seem to greatly overestimate both my powers and influence as they traverse very narrow corridors indeed. However, if it would serve to ease your anxieties, there are one or two inspectors of police of my acquaintance who might be persuaded to call in on 221b from time to time. Please be advised that your chances of hoodwinking my brother are very slim indeed but your intentions are most admirable and I fear that your motivations for such action are not entirely groundless. Egypt is a most volatile land at the best of times and I hope that my brother's inquiries do not increase those perils. He is not investigating a cosy drawing-room murder this time.'

Mycroft's enigmatic reply did nothing to allay my anxieties. I read and reread his words several times over in an effort to establish whether he was merely expressing brotherly concern or if this was a genuine warning based upon some prior knowledge of this affair. I thought the latter to be unlikely as it was well outside of his normal area of influence, although in truth I was not exactly sure what that was!

Once I had ensured that these replies were safely disposed of, I burst into Holmes's room with the news that his train to Brindisi would be departing on the following morning and mine, to Turin, some three hours later. In truth, I had booked two berths upon the Brindisi train, although mine was in third class for reasons of discretion.

That afternoon, after one final and futile inquiry at the hospital, Holmes went out to purchase a linen suit and hat, which were more suitable for the climate and terrain that he would now travel to. I secreted my own purchases within my case without Holmes's knowledge.

'You know, Watson, I cannot thank you enough for under-taking to return to London alone. There is no one I know who is better suited to the tasks that I have set for you there and no one who I could trust more. Have no fear for your old friend, I have already informed my esteemed colleague, Elraji, of my intentions, so you can be assured that I will be in safe hands.'

It seemed as if each word of his had been especially chosen with the express purpose of causing me to regret my intended deception. The pangs of conscience that they had caused almost made me give up the ghost, but the die had been cast and I was resolved to proceed.

It was decided that we would bid our farewells at the hotel, in order that I might complete my own preparations during the three-hour time lapse between our respective departures. I had advised Holmes to arrive at the station a full hour ahead of schedule as I had been reliably informed that the rail network was notoriously unpredictable.

However, despite the irritation that this further delay would undoubtedly cause Holmes, the extra hour was all that I needed in order for me to complete my subterfuge.

Once I was certain that Holmes was well set on his way to the station, I tore upstairs to my room and brought out my shaving equipment. I decided that a disguise may not always be effective because of what the victim does not expect to see but also because of what he does expect to see! Therefore, without a moment's delay, but with understandable pangs of regret, I removed my moustache.

One glance in the mirror soon convinced me that my sacrifice had not been in vain. After all, if I was finding it difficult to recognize myself without that resolute appendage, then surely Holmes would likewise fail to identify his old friend. I completed my camouflage with a pair of thick-framed spectacles and a large-brimmed soft hat that flopped across my brow. Once I had donned my new safari suit, I smiled with satisfaction as I stole one last peek in the mirror on my way to the door.

The extra hour that I had gained soon evaporated within the teeming and chaotic Roman traffic and as a consequence I arrived on the platform barely a minute before the final whistle blew! I bundled my baggage aboard and barely had time to scramble after it before the train suddenly lurched forward.

Once I had regained my composure, I realized that my first task was to attempt to locate my friend, even though I was restricted by the constraints of my third-class billet. I was fortunate in that the guards in Italy did not prove to be as vigilant as their British counterparts.

I sidled slowly towards the first-class section of the train and then positioned myself in a corridor that linked the dining car and the bathroom facilities. I was convinced that Holmes would be making use of at least one of these before too long and sure enough, my theory was soon borne out by his appearance in the corridor in front of me.

To my surprise he was heading towards the dining car and

he even appeared to be looking in my direction! However, I was soon assured of the reliability of my disguise for there was no sign of recognition on his part and he soon made his way to a seat at an empty table.

I was amused to see that Holmes refused to partake of the limited menu and instead contented himself with a pot of coffee and a cigarette, as was his wont. I kept a watchful eye while I took a light lunch and I was relieved to see him finally return to his berth.

Thankfully the journey only lasted for a little under fifteen hours, for I was not sure if I could have maintained my vigil, without going undetected, for much longer than that. Our train meandered sedately through some charming Italian countryside and we stopped occasionally at some lazy little towns such as Frosinone and the coastal town of Bari before we finally arrived at our destination.

As we alighted from the train I ensured that the rim of my hat was pulled down well over my face and I watched my friend leave the station from a discreet distance. I followed him down to the main harbour but to my dismay I soon discovered that there would not be another steamer departing for Alexandria until Sunday, which was two days hence!

Potentially, this new obstruction to our journey further jeopardized my ability to remain incognito. I observed Holmes while he made various enquiries as to the availability of accommodation and he then took directions to the nearest hotel. In this we were not to be disappointed.

For millennia Brindisi had been an important gateway between Europe and the East. Although centuries of conflict and a devastating earthquake in the eighteenth century had done much to destroy its ancient culture and architectural heritage, Brindisi still had much to offer to a discerning traveller, not least its magnificent harbour.

Therefore, Holmes and I had no great difficulty in locating

rooms close to the waterfront and I ensured that I secured a berth upon the same steamer to Alexandria as he had done. I was pleasantly surprised to see that Holmes had not decided to waste the time available to us by remaining cooped up in his room and I followed his route as he roamed from Roman columns to medieval fortresses, with enthralled interest.

I was fascinated to learn from a local that the defeated followers of Spartacus, the legendary leader of a slave revolt in the second century BC were notoriously crucified by the victorious Romans along the entire route of the Appian Way from Rome to Brindisi, the scene of his final and ill-fated battle.

All the while I managed to maintain a discreet distance and I was confident that by the time we were ready to board our steamer, the *Romulus*, Holmes was still as oblivious to my presence as he had been at the beginning of our journey. Fortunately the *Romulus* was a large enough vessel for me to be able to remain inconspicuous amongst the many passengers on board.

Once I was ensconced within my small but comfortable cabin, I made my way up to the main deck so that I could see Italy slowly fade from sight and in the hope that Holmes was doing likewise. Sure enough, I soon spotted my friend by the hand rail, shielding his pipe from the fresh Adriatic breeze, although he seemed to be more fascinated by his fellow passengers than he was by the transforming horizon that unfolded in front of us.

Two individuals, of most singular appearance, appeared to have been attracting more of his attention than the rest and in that there was no great surprise. They were both tall and heavily built and from top to toe they were dressed in the same fashion as had been our Bedouin visitor at Baker Street! On a voyage to Alexandria, their attire would not ordinarily have seemed worthy of note.

However, it was disconcerting for me to observe that they

were both reciprocating Holmes's attention and in a manner that can be best be described as obsessive and with underlying menace. Their motives were obviously unknown to me but I was certain that they were not well intentioned and I resolved to maintain a conscientious vigil for as long as they were aboard.

This promised to be for some considerable time, as the journey to Alexandria was over a distance of some 1100 nautical miles. The small steamer carried mail as well as passengers and therefore had other ports of call to make prior to our eventual arrival at Alexandria. The most notable of these was Corfu and as a result the journey lasted a full three days, despite our steady speed of twenty-two knots.

At each of these brief stops I kept an anxious eye upon both Holmes and his two earnest stalkers. However, I was disappointed to note, though not altogether surprised, that the Bedouins remained aboard the *Romulus* throughout each pause in our journey.

Upon arriving at Alexandria, I watched them all anxiously as we disembarked and I followed from an unobtrusive distance as we all made our way to the station and the next phase of our expedition. Neither Holmes nor his followers appeared to be in a particular hurry and this afforded me a few moments to reflect upon the Pillar of Pompey and the famous pink sphinx that we passed on our way from the historic harbour.

By now I had become convinced that the Bedouins would not deviate from the path that Holmes had set them upon and so I was not particularly overwhelmed when I heard them arrange tickets for Cairo at the booking office. Indeed, I would have been more surprised had they not done so.

However, we soon discovered that there would not be a train going to Cairo for another two full days and, once again, I found myself following Holmes to yet another hotel, only this time I was not alone!

Despite the irritation that this delay would undoubtedly cause Holmes, I consoled myself with the realization that I had now had the opportunity to reopen my lines of communication with London. At once I despatched wires to both 221b and the Diogenes club, informing both recipients of my temporary forwarding address. All that remained for me to do was anxiously await their replies.

Come the evening, I was relieved to find that Holmes had decided to make use of the hotel's dining room. There had been precious little of an edible nature on the boat, so consequently I was absolutely famished by supper time.

Once again I was astonished to see that Holmes was able to function without the intake of nutrition that normal human beings seem to require. He had hardly touched his food and I had barely time to finish my own meal before he extinguished his cigarette and hurried from the room. I made sure that Holmes was securely locked in his room before I retired to my own.

The next morning the Bedouins and I followed Holmes to the large local market, otherwise known as the bazaar, where he examined a countless number of large-rimmed, linen hats. Once he had made his selection he turned his attention to the dazzling array of fruits and vegetables that were piled up high upon dozens of small carts around the market's perimeter.

The hustle and bustle of the place was both invigorating and deafening. There were brightly dressed vendors, each of whom had distinctive and individual calls as they sought to bring the attention of the passers-by to their merchandise. Many of the customers were equally loud and vociferous as they went about the task of bartering down the price of their chosen item. Cutting a huge swathe through the middle of this commotion rode a constant flow of camels, each one moving slowly under the burden of cloth, wood and straw and burly drivers with their whips.

Dozens of wizened, elderly women led their donkeys by the bridle in front of small wooden carts crammed with merchandise. However, the most eye-catching sight seemed to be the conspicuously large number of aloof European tourists who were milling around in their search for a ridiculous bargain.

The women wore shaded headwear and carried light-coloured parasols, although I smiled at the sight of those who refused to surrender their bustles, even in the face of such glaring and oppressive heat! Likewise, several of the gentlemen would not yield up their top hats, although the vast majority were dressed more practically.

At that moment, seemingly from the very centre of this maelstrom of colour and noise, emerged a man who actually stood out, even in the midst of this vast cacophony! He was exceptionally tall and thin, he stood at least six feet four and made Holmes appear as positively bulky. He was dressed in a very smart charcoal-grey, European-style suit and yet upon his head he wore a keffiyeh, the traditional headwear of the Bedouins. He sported a most luxuriant jet-black moustache and his bearing had a military erectness that was unmistakable.

When he walked it was with an arrogant authority but then I realized, when it was almost too late, that this stranger was walking directly towards Holmes! In an instant I made towards the two of them, ready to intervene should ensuing events oblige me to. My hand automatically wrapped itself around my army revolver which was secreted within my jacket pocket, while my finger readied the trigger.

The stranger continued towards Holmes without hesitation. I studied his eyes for any indications of a deadly intent, while Holmes remained oblivious to his approach. I was on the point of betraying my identity and withdrawing my revolver when to my great surprise and not a little relief both Holmes and the stranger extended their hands out to each other and shook them with a friendly enthusiasm.

They immediately fell into an intense and guarded conference. Soon the stranger, who was clearly familiar with the ways of the bazaar, led Holmes stealthily away from the centre of the pandemonium and towards a small hookah den, or as we call them, shisha lounge, which was draped with brightly coloured and luxuriant textiles.

Here they smoked tobacco, cooled by the water in the bowl of the hookah and drank copious amounts of Turkish coffee, while they engaged in an intense conversation. By now I was satisfied that that this new companion of Holmes was none other than his highly regarded correspondent Elraji. However, I could not be sure, at this point, why Holmes had kept me ignorant of Elraji's reply to the wire that he had sent him while we were still in London.

Nevertheless, the sight of them together allowed me to relax for the very first time since we had departed from Rome. Then a thought suddenly occurred to me and sure enough, as I gazed around intently, I realized that the two Bedouins, who had been dogging our every step, were now nowhere to be seen!

Evidently Elraji and his profession was well known to them and the very sight of him had sent them scurrying for cover. Of course, the meaning of this was clear and I was now in little doubt that those resolute hunters had no good motives behind their actions. However, I was equally certain that we had not seen the last of them, by any means.

With their conference at an end, Elraji walked with Holmes to the hotel and they shook hands again outside the entrance before Elraji took his leave. Sure enough, within a moment of his departure, our persistent followers re-emerged.

This was a pattern that would repeat itself the following day as we all made our way towards the train to Cairo. Mercifully, this, the final stage of our journey, was also the shortest and within five hours of steady but uncomfortable progress, we emerged within the centre of the old town of Cairo.

By a stroke of good fortune my replies from London had arrived at the hotel just minutes before we had made our final departure. Mrs Hudson had confirmed that she had followed my advice and instructions to the letter, while Mycroft assured me that our old friend, Inspector Gregson of Scotland Yard, had kept a very watchful eye upon our landlady these past few days.

I was enormously relieved to receive this news. Inspector Gregson, although not the sharpest detective on the force, was certainly the most tenacious and thorough officer that you could hope for. He had also confirmed to Mycroft that there had been no further sign of our blustering Bedouin friend and that Mrs Hudson remained quite safe.

I must confess that this news went some way towards dispelling the pangs of guilt that had been haunting me from the moment that I had put into motion the seemingly impossible task of deceiving Sherlock Holmes!

CHAPTER NINE

A SACRED ALLY

THE SCENE THAT greeted us as we emerged once more into the searing and merciless sunlight was reminiscent of the one that we had experienced in the centre of Alexandria. This time, however, the sights and the sounds were of a volume that was ten times greater than before!

I frequently dabbed at the sweat upon my forehead with a white handkerchief that was rapidly turning grey. There was no respite from the heat nor could we find the blessed sanctuary of shade. However, at least I could take some consolation from the fact that Holmes and Elraji clearly had no intention of lingering here for any longer than they had to.

There was certainly more urgency and intent in Holmes's stride now and I watched from a close distance as they jostled and shoved their way towards the perimeter of the teeming crowds. For now, at least, there was no sight of the Bedouins so I could concentrate on the task of keeping Holmes clearly within my sight.

Holmes's knowledge of the streets of old Cairo were as limited as my own, so we were both very much in the hands of Elraji whose progress was unrelenting. Gradually the crowds began to thin and before too long I realized, with a thrill, that he was leading us towards the sweeping majesty that was the River Nile!

Of course, our final destination still very much remained a mystery. Perhaps even more incomprehensible to me was the true reason behind our making this journey in the first place. Nevertheless, with every step that we took I could feel the breeze that drifted towards us from that broad expanse of water gradually increase and I knew that before too long I would be standing upon the banks of a river that once sustained a great nation and helped to forge a mighty empire.

The magnificent mosques and the ancient churches that lined our route sadly flashed past us in a dizzying blur. We were constantly being called to and berated by the many people that we barged into as we made our urgent progress towards the river. The sight that greeted us, when we did finally arrive at its bank, simply took my breath away.

The breadth – it is a full half-mile across at its widest – and the grandeur of this legendary river surely qualified it as one of the natural wonders of the world and I could now understand why the pharaohs and their priests worshipped it as a god in its own right. However, I could not afford to linger for too long upon such thoughts, for I suddenly realized that Holmes and Elraji were busy engaging the services of one of the many small feluccas that were moored around a jetty just below us.

I was also conscious of the fact that with the crowds of people now having thinned appreciably, my own presence was certainly becoming more conspicuous. As it happened, so was the absence of our Bedouin friends. Obviously I could not afford to be seen rushing towards the jetty in the wake of Holmes and Elraji, so I strolled casually along the dirt track that led to it in the hope that I might discover their intended destination from the numerous pilots that were gathered around their boats.

This plan was all very well, until I realized that English was not a language commonly used by these simple boat men. I was on the point of despair as I watched Holmes and Elraji slowly sail away into the distance, when a deep baritone voice boomed towards me from the deck of a felucca.[1] 'I might be able to help you, Englishman,' the man proposed as he walked towards me. There was a mischievous glint in his eye which told me that he certainly could help me, but only for a price.

The voice belonged to a descendant of the ancient and once-feared people known as the Nubians. He cut an imposing figure as he stood with legs astride upon the deck of his small vessel, clothed in his people's traditional dress, a white Galabeya. He broke into the broadest grin, exposing a mass of white teeth that almost blinded me in the glare of the sun. He made it up to the deck of the jetty with a single gigantic stride and I found him towering over me when I next heard that amazing voice.

'I am sure that I can help you, Englishman. You are constantly looking anxiously after the boat that is slowly edging its way upstream, with another Englishman on board and the policeman, are you not?' the Nubian asked, and he was apparently already certain of my answer.

'How did you know about the policeman and my intentions?' I asked.

'Be quick with your decision, Englishman, for soon they will be too far away for even I to be able to reel them in!' he proclaimed.

Under a different set of circumstances I might have been infuriated by the manner of his haughty declaration. However, I found there to be something quite agreeable about his self-confidence and of course he was quite right, the distance between Holmes and I was increasing with each passing moment.

The Nubian and I agreed a price and within a very short time he and I had soon clambered aboard and the felucca was on its way.

'You are indeed fortunate today, Englishman, for there is no other boatman on the Nile who understands its currents and its winds as well as I. We shall catch them, I assure you,' he declared with another broad smile.

I then had to explain to him that I did not wish ours to overtake the other boat but merely to remain within clear eyeshot. He acknowledged his compliance with a knowing smile and at once he applied less intensity to his handling of the rigging.

Our vessel was little more than forty feet in length and its streamlined hull and short berth meant that it was ideally designed to skim the rippling waves and take advantage of the undercurrents in the hands of a skilled pilot. The Nubian surely was the boatman that he had declared himself to be and as our elegant wooden boat, of ancient design, glided gracefully along that magnificent river, I gazed across at him in admiration at his handling of the single, lateen cotton sail.

Consequently, we were visibly gaining ground on Holmes's felucca. In my dreams I had visualized a journey to the wonders of ancient Egypt a dozen times or more. However, I had always imagined that my progress from Cairo would have been at the more sedate pace of a donkey or camel, allowing me time to marvel at the many wonders that adorned our route.

The island of Rhoda, the seat of the gigantic, measuring obelisk known as the Nilometer, seemed to disappear in an instant. I was even more aghast once I realized that the famous pyramids of Giza were only a relative stone's throw away from the opposite bank to our eventual destination, but for the time being they would remain tantalizingly out of reach to me.

Instead I turned my attention to the boat ahead of us. Evidently speed had been Holmes's motivation in selecting this mode of transport and I became concerned that I would lose sight of him by the time that our boat finally tied up at the jetty. At that moment the insightful Nubian proved his worth to me still further.

'Englishman, you may be interested to learn that I overheard the conversation between the policeman and the master of the other boat,' he informed me, with another winning smile, knowing full well how I was going to respond.

'Well, of course I am interested!' I declared. 'Although I am afraid that before you divulge its contents, I might have to fill your coffers still further.'

The Nubian shrugged his gigantic shoulders.

'Englishman, I am but a humble boatman and a very poor man. Besides, I am sure that you will find your quarry without my aid. See how they are already climbing away from the jetty and out of sight. It is a pity to have come all of this way only to lose your goal at the end of the journey.' He sang to himself quietly and nonchalantly as he began to ease his vessel towards the bank.

Sure enough, Holmes and Elraji were already moving out of sight, despite the fact that my skilled boatman had managed to negotiate the five-mile journey in a little under an hour. As we drew closer to the jetty, with a smile that I could barely suppress, I pressed a note into the palm of the Nubian's hand.

'Englishman, you are surely as wise as you are generous,' he responded patronizingly. 'I will tell you all that you need to know.'

He beckoned me to wait for a few moments longer while he expertly piloted his felucca to the jetty and safely secured it. He then leant towards me and whispered into my ear.

'You will find your friend within the walls of al-Muallaqah,' he said enigmatically.

'What, pray, is the meaning of that and how do you know that it is a friend that I seek?'

'When you reach the top of the bank merely ask any passer-by for directions to the Hanging Church. I watched your eyes during our pursuit and I could see anxiety within them but no dark intent. Now, no more questions, Englishman!' he boomed.

'Nubian, you are surely as wise as you are voracious!' I responded with a laugh. We clasped arms as I finally went ashore and I watched him for a moment as he shared a gourd of wine with his crewman before instructing him to unfetter the rope and make for a speedy return to Cairo.

I climbed the same path that I had seen Holmes set upon but a few moments before. Then, to my surprise, I found myself pausing to look out upon that vast and timeless river as I lit a cigarette. Perhaps, now that I had almost reached my journey's end and knew of Holmes's exact location, it was for the first time in many days that I felt no real need of urgency.

I watched the Nubian's felucca glide majestically up the river, as so many had done before her over the millennia. I gazed longingly towards the opposite bank in the sure knowledge that behind the imposing sand dunes stood the last of the seven wonders of the ancient world, namely the pyramids of Giza.

It was then, however, that I saw something that changed my brief moment of repose into an instant of stark horror. For surely there was Elraji engaging a felucca of his own for a return journey to Cairo! I shuddered at the thought of a similar realization that I once had at the Reichenbach Falls and I threw away my cigarette as I scrambled frantically up the sandy bank.

As the Nubian had predicted, I had no great difficulty in obtaining accurate directions to the Hanging Church and moved with all speed. I would subsequently discover the reason behind the church's unusual title, in that it was built by being suspended over the columns of a Roman fort known as 'The Towers of Babylon'. However, the meaning behind its other designation, the Staircase Church, was made known to me as soon as I began my breathless ascent of the twenty-nine, wide stone steps that led to its only entrance.

I searched around every niche and sanctuary within that ancient Coptic church, until with dismay and a pounding heart I realized that the Nubian had seriously misled me: in error, I hoped. It was as if my entire journey and my foul deception of Holmes had been totally in vain. I was distraught.

I wandered haplessly and listlessly back down that gigantic staircase and I then began a fruitless search around its vast perimeter. Now convinced that all was lost, I sank down upon the remains of a sandstone wall, lit up a cigarette and began to weigh up my options, if indeed I still had any.

Of course, I could engage in a search of the surrounding neighbourhood: after all, an Englishman here would be far more conspicuous than one on the far side of the Nile. Alternatively, I might seek an immediate return berth to Cairo, in the hope that I could locate Elraji and discover Holmes's whereabouts from him.

The time involved in the second alternative was certainly prohibitive, especially as I was no more certain of its success as I was of the former. Elraji might have had his own reasons for returning to Cairo and know nothing of Holmes's subsequent intentions and fate. I was determined that if I was to be of any use to Holmes, it would have to be here and now.

I threw my cigarette away with a determined sweep of my arm and I was now resolved to scouring every building and sifting through each grain of sand, until my quest was complete. Despite the obvious barrier of language, I approached two sun-baked nomads who were tending to their camels close by.

'Have you seen a tall Englishman?' I called out desperately while pointing to my eyes and then to the top of my head. They merely shrugged their shoulders apathetically and continued with the grooming of their remarkable beasts. I turned away from them and continued with my search.

'Really, Watson, I am surprised that my simple stratagem of applying a robe and a change of headwear could have taken in such a seasoned traveller and a master of disguises!'

I could hardly believe my ears. It was that familiar voice that I had longed to hear the most and yet, in my heart of hearts, had least expected to hear. Dare I turn around and face its source, or had the intense heat induced in me a form of brain fever? My mind was made up for me by the sound of a riotous, strident burst of laughter that left me in little doubt as to its owner.

By the time that I had turned around, the robe and headwear had been removed and there, dressed in the linen suit and hat that I had last seen him in, stood my very good friend, Sherlock Holmes!

He greeted me with the broadest and warmest of smiles and he walked towards me with an outstretched hand. I was overwhelmed by a feeling of intense relief at the sight of him standing there, perfectly well and mercifully unharmed. Consequently, I was on the point of reciprocating when an uncomfortable thought occurred to me.

'My dear fellow, naturally I am overjoyed at the sight of you standing there as fit and as well as ever I have seen you. However, I am yearning to know how long it has been since you became aware of my deception and my presence?'

Holmes was visibly taken aback by the directness of my question, and he turned his face away as if he was afraid of it betraying his sense of embarrassment. He beckoned for me to join him upon the ruined section of wall that I had been occupying but a few moments before.

'You must understand, Watson, that if I had betrayed your presence at any stage of our journey earlier than this, it would have seriously compromised my ability to travel with as much discretion and freedom as I was able to. Naturally, once I became aware of the close attentions of our Bedouin friends, it became even more important to me that you maintained a close but discreet attendance, especially upon those stages of the journey before I was met by my old friend Elraji.'

'Ah, so I was right, that was he!'

'Yes, Watson. He has returned to Cairo to continue with certain inquiries on my behalf, although I anticipate that you should be able to meet him within a day or two.' Holmes became aware, from my raised eyebrow, that I was still insisting upon an answer to my original enquiry.

'Naturally you will be interested to know that I recognized my Watson from that moment when we almost collided with each other in the dining car. Up to that moment, I assure you, I was still convinced that you were making your way to London on my behalf.'

'But that incident occurred on the train from Rome!' I was horrified to realize that I had been found out at such an early stage of my plan.

'Do not scold yourself too harshly, Doctor. After all, I would be a very poor detective indeed were I not able to recognize a man with whom I have shared so much over so many years, merely from the removal of a piece of facial hair and a change of hat!' Holmes was right, of course; I had been pushing the bounds of credibility too far in presuming to deceive a man of Holmes's acute observational abilities.

'Yet you have used me, Holmes, and jeopardized the safety of Mrs Hudson by not declaring your hand at an earlier opportunity! Surely you have gone too far this time?'

'No more so than you, friend Watson. You will be able to confirm, quite easily, that I too sent similar wires to both my brother and Mrs Hudson and would not have proceeded had I not received reassuring replies from both.' I smiled at Holmes's attempts at placating me.

'Well, you certainly seem to have an answer for everything, I must say! Perhaps you will now tell me how you intend to proceed from this point onwards?'

Holmes stood up suddenly and pointed towards the ancient church that rose majestically behind us.

'My friend and colleague, Elraji, has suggested that we begin our quest here, on the site of one of the oldest churches in existence. For it was from within these sacred walls that the scrolls, whose secrets we seek, were originally stolen!'

I followed Holmes's gaze intently but soon became aware of a large bowl of dust that seemed to be moving in our direction with some intent and at great speed. I had heard of such phenomena before, sandstorms created by an unusually high increase in air pressure and extraordinary high land temperatures. I had even experienced them myself during the course of the dry season in my time in Afghanistan.

However, this one appeared to be smaller and considerably faster than any of my experience and it appeared to be moving directly towards us! As yet Holmes was not aware of the presence of this apparition. His back was turned towards its approach and he began to walk slowly towards the base of that gigantic staircase.

I was transfixed by the extraordinary movement of the dust cloud. So transfixed, in fact, that it was almost upon us before it began to dispel and its centre was then revealed to me. Two marauding Bedouin horsemen were charging down upon us with their swords raised menacingly above their heads as if ready to strike!

It was only then that I realized that the attack was aimed solely towards Holmes, who was only alerted to the imminent danger by my immediate and repeated call of warning. At the last, I flung myself towards him in the most successful rugby tackle that I had ever executed and Holmes landed on his face barely inches away from near certain death.

The margin was so narrow that, as I landed on the ground just behind Holmes, my right shoulder was caught by a trailing hoof. I was back on my feet but an instant later and I released a couple of rounds from my army revolver in the direction of our attackers. They were driving their mounts at such a speed that I did not reasonably expect to achieve any accuracy with those shots over such a distance. However, I had hoped that by firing towards them I might have deterred them from returning with a renewed attack and in that, at least, I proved to be successful.

Holmes and I dusted ourselves down slowly and in silence for a few moments and I was relieved to discover that my shoulder had suffered nothing more serious than a light bruising and a small graze.

'You have suffered an injury on my behalf,' Holmes stated simply, quietly and without emotion.

'It is nothing of note, I assure you, Holmes. It is a graze and nothing more. Have you escaped injury?' I asked anxiously.

'Indeed I have, apart from the damage to my pride!' Holmes exclaimed unexpectedly.

'Whatever do you mean?'

'I certainly should have been more vigilant and realized that the likelihood of an attack of this nature was not entirely without credence. I fancy that the effects of my oversight would have been a good deal more injurious had it not been for the timely intervention of the ever-attentive Doctor Watson! However, although I am glad that you did so on this occasion, I would still not advocate that you disregard all of my future instructions,'

'Holmes, you can be assured that I would never contemplate such a course of action again, unless it was under the most extreme of circumstances,' I confirmed.

As we stood up again I noticed that Holmes's eyes were being drawn once again towards the top of the staircase that led to the Hanging Church. More specifically, I should add, towards a small, solitary figure, who stood upon the upper-most step. He was dressed in the simple black robes of a Coptic priest, which was made all the more recognizable by the Coptic cross that was emblazoned upon it. This was a symbol with which I was gradually becoming all the more familiar as the case steadily progressed.

The priest gestured for us to join him and even though his face was shrouded by a large black hood that was pulled down, we could tell that this was a friendly gesture. We wasted no time in responding to his invitation and Holmes attempted to take the steps two at a time.

'Come along, Watson, there really is no time to lose!' he called down to me as I began the long climb.

By the time that I had breathlessly reached the top of the stairs, Holmes and the priest had already disappeared into the dark and deliciously cool interior. I paused for a moment to marvel at the intricately decorated wooden doors, although the exact meaning of those complex geometric patterns I was never to discover. However, there was no mistaking the distinctive Coptic crosses that liberally adorned the doors and walls.

I was gazing in wonder at the thirteen columns that supported the marble pulpit when Holmes whispered to me from behind a sanctuary screen in the oldest section of the church. I followed his hushed voice and soon found him seated at a low table next to the aged priest whom we had noticed at the top of the stairs.

As far as I could tell, we three were currently the only occupants of the church. However, we continued to speak with whispered tones as the stone floors and marble columns produced a marked echo effect. By now the sun was beginning to sink below the horizon, so the priest proceeded to light many long candles before he rejoined Holmes and me at the table. He then produced an earthenware carafe from which he poured out three large goblets of wine.

To my surprise the priest spoke remarkably good English.

'Gentlemen, I know from Elraji your reasons for seeking me out and we have much to discuss. First of all we drink!' he pronounced and we saluted each other by raising our goblets. 'Drain your cups, gentlemen, for the carafe is surprisingly deep.' We gladly followed his bidding as the wine was cool and absolutely delicious.

'Watson, allow me to introduce you to Shenouda, the holy representative of Pope Cyril V of Alexandria and the Coptic Patriarch of all Africa and the Holy See of Saint Mark. As you might also have gathered, he has liaised extensively with Elraji regarding the theft of the infamous and bloodstained Gospel which was removed from this very church. In our search for the truth he will become our closest ally, so listen well.'

Shenouda refilled our goblets, however, I supped from mine with rather less enthusiasm than I had before for by now I had no doubt that our discussions would continue well into the night and I was already a little weary.

CHAPTER TEN

THE LAST OF THE FEW

ALTHOUGH PERHAPS NOT pertinent to the matter at hand, at the very outset Shenouda furnished us with a fascinating insight into the history and structure of the Coptic Church.

It is generally regarded that the Coptic Church was the first to have been established, not only in Egypt, but anywhere in the world. The Apostle, Saint Mark, arrived in Egypt in 41 AD and immediately set about the task of establishing Christianity as the majority religion in Egypt as it remained right up to the time of the Muslim conquest. Even today there are an estimated ten million Copts still practising their religion there.

However, as with many religions, amongst the Copts there are countless variations in theologies and as a consequence a schism was formed, in the early part of this century, which led to the creation of the Patriarchate of Coptic Catholics. The most obvious variant between the beliefs of the two Patriarchs is the full communion that exists between the Coptic Catholics led by Kyrillos Makarios and the Pope of Rome.

'Mark that well, Watson, for I am certain that it is a fact of the utmost significance.' Holmes broke in upon Shenouda's summary in a state of great excitement.

I became curious as to the appearance of the aged priest beneath his spacious hood. As if sensing this, Shenouda suddenly bared his head and revealed a surprisingly full head of flowing white locks. His sharp grey eyes seemed to pierce me to my very soul and when he smiled it was with a warmth that was born of wisdom and compassion. His skin, which had been seasoned by a lifetime of exposure to some of the most intense sunlight on the planet, was deeply lined and appeared to be of the same texture as the papyrus that we had come to seek advice upon.

'Mr Holmes, Elraji has informed me about your great wisdom and of that I am in little doubt. You are quite correct; the rivalry between the two Patriarchs has enormous bearing upon the fate of the missing Gospel. Perhaps once I have explained to you the startling contents of this Gospel you will fully understand the reason why.'

'Before you do so, it would be of enormous benefit if you could explain to us the exact circumstances and events that led to the theft of this most singular of documents,' Holmes quietly requested.

The aged priest responded immediately by standing up and then moving towards a small sanctuary above the southern bastion. This is considered to be the only original fragment of the earliest church to have survived the ravages of centuries of war and natural disasters. Shenouda encouraged us to join him by smiling and crooking his finger. We followed him into a small crypt and there he showed us a motley collection of holy relics pertaining to Saint Mark and a small recess that once contained the Gospel of Mary Magdalene!

'Mary Magdalene?' I exclaimed. 'I had no idea that such a thing existed.'

'I am not surprised at that, Doctor Watson. For millennia it has been one of our most cherished of treasures, but prior to recent events, we were certain that there was no knowledge of its existence outside of our enclave,' Shenouda responded.

'Well, you certainly did not go to any great lengths in protecting or concealing so important an object,' Holmes observed disdainfully.

'Mr Holmes, we were confident that ignorance of its presence here was protection enough. This is a house of God and we had faith in the safety of this sanctuary. Sadly, in that we were very much mistaken.' Shenouda shook his head solemnly as he lamented the loss of such a precious object before leading us back to the small table and chairs.

We all drank deeply from our goblets before Holmes encouraged Shenouda to continue with his account of the theft.

'Who would carry out such a heinous crime and what could possibly have been the motive behind such an obscure theft?' I asked incredulously.

'The object might very well be an obscure one, Doctor Watson, but that does not necessarily mean that it has little value, or significance. For example, consider the intense rivalry that exists between my Patriarch, Cyril V, and Makarios, of the Coptic Catholics. I assure you gentlemen that Makarios seeks for nothing less than the total absorption of the Orthodox Church within the auspices of the Coptic Catholics, with Makarios eventually becoming the leader of every Copt in Africa!

'Once I have outlined to you the contents of the Gospel of Mary Magdalene, you will fully understand why the Pope in Rome would wholeheartedly sanction and approve such an amalgamation and the dissolution of the Coptic Orthodox Church. If they have their way, Pope Cyril V will surely become its last ever Patriarch.'

'Are the contents of this Gospel so extreme that you think this eventuality to be likely?' Holmes asked with some concern.

'Yes, I am certain of it. Furthermore, knowing that he has the full sanction of the Pope of Rome, Makarios has made no effort at concealing his ambitions. I have explained to you the motive behind the crime, but the identity of the thief is a little bit more obscure. Elraji is in no doubt that the Gospel was removed by an infamous dealer of antiquities who goes by the name of Hashmoukh. However, Hashmoukh is nothing more than a minor player within the framework of a far bigger game!'

Those last words of Shenouda seemed to light a flame behind the previously docile eyes of my friend. He could barely conceal a smile of anticipation and he jumped up out of his chair with a cigarette in his hand. Shenouda shook his head in disapproval, so Holmes immediately excused himself before going back outside to smoke. I decided to join him.

'Holmes, surely a man of the cloth like Cardinal Tosca would not have sanctioned the theft of a holy relic from another church, even one of another denomination?' I asked as soon as we emerged into the twilight. 'Besides, what possible connection could Tosca have had with a man of Hashmoukh's dubious reputation?'

Holmes raised an eyebrow 'Ah, Watson, you are making the assumption that such a connection existed. I think it to be far more likely that the Gospel was offered to Tosca based upon his scholarly reputation. Shenouda spoke of a far bigger game and there could not possibly be a bigger player than a man who is widely regarded as the next Pope of Rome!'

As usual I could not find a fault in Holmes's reasoning and a moment later we rejoined Shenouda inside the church.

'Who else, other than Hashmoukh, would have had knowledge of the Gospel's existence? Makarios, perhaps?' Holmes suggested, before Shenouda had a chance to continue with his story.

'Oh no, Mr Holmes, were that true it would have disappeared from our church long ago and he would have used it for his own nefarious schemes by now,' Shenouda replied with some surprise in his voice.

'Yet a moment ago you spoke of a bigger game. Surely that implies that Hashmoukh did not carry out the theft on his own behalf,' I speculated.

Shenouda laughed at the very idea.

'Doctor Watson, the recent and startling increase in the number of European tourists and archaeologists to our country has resulted in a massive interest in ancient Egyptian artefacts. Therefore, those who are neither clever nor industrious enough to procure such treasures by their own efforts, but have the wealth enabling them to purchase such things, enlist the aid of someone like Hashmoukh.

'Unscrupulous dealers and thieves think nothing of the rape of their own country's heritage in their desire to line their own pockets and thereby satisfy the passion of European collectors. I assure you that, within a few days of its theft, the Gospel of Mary Magdalene had become nothing more than a small part of a vast collection of stolen antiquities in one of the great houses of Europe.'

'I suppose, therefore, that its disappearance from the desk of Cardinal Tosca within the Vatican is inexplicable to you?' Holmes surmised.

'Oh, absolutely, Mr Holmes. Hashmoukh normally conducts his business from the place of his birth, Akhmim, which is a small town on the banks of the River Nile. From there he circulates word of his latest acquisitions to his many clients and, of course, he will then sell to the highest bidder. Of late his keenest client has been the fervent collector and celebrated theologian, Professor Ronald Sydney of London—'

'London?' I blurted out. I could not help myself from interrupting the aged priest because the mere mention of London immediately brought to mind the nationality of Inspector Gialli's brutal attackers. I apologized at once for my rudeness.

'I understand your surprise, Doctor Watson. You have travelled a long and hard journey only to discover that a clue to your mystery may exist within the town that you left behind you so long ago. Now the question is how did the murderer of Cardinal Tosca know of the presence of the Gospel upon his desk and then understand its contents sufficiently for him to be able discriminate between the important passages of text and the trivial?' Shenouda put this to Holmes and I in a manner that suggested he had a theory of his own.

Holmes raised a quizzical eyebrow in Shenouda's direction and then smiled when he recognized the old man's perceptiveness.

'I am certain that once I have the answer to that question two mysteries will be solved at once,' Holmes responded thoughtfully. 'You have been of immeasurable assistance in this matter, yet I need one last service from you. A summary of the contents of the Gospel will go some way to pointing me in the right direction, I am sure.'

'Oh, Mr Holmes, I am an old man, the hour is late and the matter is not a brief or trifling one. There is a sparse though comfortable room close to my own at the rear of the church. I suggest that you take some much-needed rest and we shall resume in the morning. Do not be troubled, for I am a very early riser!'

To my surprise, Holmes accepted Shenouda's offer gratefully and without objection. We stepped outside for our final pipe before following Shenouda along a veritable labyrinth of dark, sand stone corridors to our room.

In one respect Shenouda's description had been an accurate one: the room was indeed sparse, but it was certainly not comfortable! Our beds might as well have been made of stone and I was amazed at how swiftly and completely Holmes fell into a deep sleep. His mind had been exercised to its fullest extent and yet his greatest challenges still lay ahead.

Shenouda had been as good as his word and he arrived at our door the following morning while the Egyptian sun was still labouring to climb above the timeless horizon. He presented us with bowls of a coarse porridge made from the local corn and then once they were consumed he suggested that we continue with our discussion while taking a bracing walk along the banks of the Nile.

We were surprised when Shenouda draped himself repeatedly with a warm woollen cloth, but soon realized that at that time of day the Nile breezes would easily find their way through the fabric of our linen suits. Shenouda smiled knowingly at the sight of Holmes and I shuddering in the cold and hurriedly closing every button on our jackets.

'I am afraid that the sand does not retain the heat and the vast waters cool the air,' he explained.

We walked in silence for a half mile or so and as the rising sun began to make its presence felt, we sank to the ground beneath the shelter of a small cluster of lush palm trees.

'It is no surprise to me that, prior to the events that you are now investigating; you had no knowledge of the existence of the Gospel of Mary Magdalene. It is one of the most closely guarded secrets within the Christian community and there are many who would hope that it remain so,' Shenouda began.

Holmes leant back against the trunk of one of the trees, lit a pipe and closed his eyes in concentration, for he now knew that Shenouda was about to expand upon what he surely regarded as the crucial element of this affair.

'Although it is generally accepted that it is the four recognized Gospels that form the basis of the New Testament, there are other writings from the same period that deserve as much interest and attention. The Apocryphon of John, the Act of Peter and the Gospel of Thomas are prime examples of these.

'They form a part of what is known as the "Coptic Codex", ancient Christian writings, probably written in the early part of the second century AD in the ancient Coptic language and then, in the fifth century, they were translated into Greek, the primary scholastic language of the time. They have gradually disappeared from circulation, partially due to neglect and potentially due to suppression on the basis that their authenticity has frequently been brought into question.

'The Gospel of Mary Magdalene is also part of this Codex, but it is unique in that, to date, no copy in Greek has ever come to light. The obvious conclusion to draw is that this Gospel has undoubtedly been actively suppressed over a period of many hundreds of years. The question that you require an answer to, Mr Holmes, is why has it been suppressed and by whom?' Shenouda paused for a moment while he studied my friend's face to gauge the impact that his statement had made upon him.

Holmes's countenance remained as inscrutable as ever, but Shenouda smiled when he observed him arch his left eyebrow and pull upon his pipe. I could not, however, maintain my silence.

'It seems to me that the Gospel of Mary Magdalene was suppressed for reasons other than its lack of authenticity. Who is the judge of its validity? Cardinal Tosca, perhaps?' I noticed Holmes smile proudly at the significance of my question and we all stood up again at the suggestion of Shenouda.

'At my age it has become increasingly difficult for me to maintain my legs in such a position for any length of time,' he explained and we continued with our sedate stroll along the river's edge.

I was beginning to think that my question had been long forgotten by both Holmes and the priest, when Shenouda began to expand upon the contents of the mysterious Gospel.

'Doctor Watson, I think it highly unlikely that Cardinal Tosca would have been the decision maker in this matter. If that had been the case, I am in little doubt that it would have been destroyed long before it was stolen from his desk! Cardinal Tosca has long held the reputation of being of a scholastic turn of mind with a passion for studying ancient texts and manuscripts that pertain to the early church. I am certain that it is for that reason alone that the Gospel was first offered to him,' Shenouda explained.

'Even at the risk of Hashmoukh antagonizing and disappointing his most regular and valued client, Professor Ronald Sydney?' Holmes asked.

'The Vatican is by no means an impoverished institution, Mr Holmes, and there is no code of loyalty for people like Hashmoukh. For someone like him it is all about obtaining the highest price that he can.'

'I can understand why a scholar such as Cardinal Tosca would attach so much importance and value to such an artefact, but I cannot comprehend why anybody should wish to destroy so priceless a relic,' I ventured.

'I am an old man, Doctor Watson, and my memory is not what it once was. However, I will try to summarize what I can recall of the contents of the Gospel in the hope that recent events will then become a little clearer to you. In brief then, the Gospel of Mary Magdalene, were its contents to become part of the public domain, would undoubtedly tear asunder the very fabric of the Roman Catholic Church!' Shenouda held up his hand in an effort at holding back the inevitable deluge of questions that he was expecting from Holmes and me.

'In order to understand the Gospel's significance you must

attempt to shed every accepted concept that you might hold,' the priest continued.

'I am sorry, but I do not understand.' I was not certain if it was the effect of the rapidly rising sun and its increasing heat, or perhaps it was the intoxicating nature of Shenouda's words, but at that very moment my head began to reel to dizzying effect and I almost fell to the sand as if concussed. From beneath his robe Shenouda immediately produced a gourd brimming over with deliciously cool water which he allowed me to drink from feverously.

Holmes looked down upon me with some concern while he waited for me to recover. Thankfully he did not have to wait for very long as the water had a rejuvenating effect upon me that was almost immediate. I thanked Shenouda for his ministrations and bade him to continue with his summary of the Gospel of Mary Magdalene.

'For us to be able to comprehend why there are certain people who might regard the publication of this Gospel to be a highly dangerous and pervasive act, we must first consider the structure of the Roman Catholic Church as it exists today and consequently forget the teachings of the early Christian Church.

'Obviously, the most significant block on which the majority of this edifice is built, is the fact that every Pope since the time of Peter is proclaimed to be his direct spiritual successor. This holy lineage is based upon the belief that Peter was the first of the Apostles to witness the risen Christ and then he was also declared, within the Gospel of Matthew, to be Christ's chosen successor and the founding rock upon which his future church would be built.

'Peter's position within the Church was consolidated from the moment that he was crucified for providing comfort to the martyrs who were being slaughtered by the Emperor Nero in Rome. The fact that his crucifixion was carried out

upon Vatican Hill consequently led to Rome and more specifically, the Vatican itself, being confirmed as the centre of the
Christian world.'

By now the sun had almost reached the height of its powers
and Shenouda decided to sacrifice the comfort of being able to
stretch his legs in favour of the luxury of the shade of our tree.
I could sense Holmes's growing impatience and frustration
and despite his undoubted respect for our spiritual guide, he
now found that he could contain himself no longer.

'As fascinating as your insight into the structure of the
Roman Catholic Church surely is, the urgency of our friend's
situation in Rome now requires that we focus more upon
the matter at hand and less upon a theological discourse!' I
was shocked and surprised by Holmes's verbal attack upon
a man who had shown us only kindness and consideration.
Shenouda did not appear to be so dismayed at Holmes's out-
burst and he laughed softly to himself.

'Mr Holmes, I see that your undoubted wisdom does not
also extend to patience and understanding. The background
that I have just outlined to you was entirely necessary if you
are to appreciate, in any intelligent way, the significance of
Mary's Gospel and the threat that its publication poses to the
accepted order of things.'

'You also mentioned the irrelevance of the early Christian
teachings. Are the two connected?' Holmes accepted
Shenouda's mild rebuke with a wry smile and he asked this
question with great respect.

'Oh yes, Mr Holmes, the threat posed by the publication of
this Gospel is not just restricted to the Catholic Church. The
entire fabric of our society would be under threat were the
contents of the Gospel to fall into the wrong hands!' Shenouda
declared dramatically.

'To whom do those hands belong?'

'Oh, Mr Holmes, now you are taking me outside of my

usual area of providence. That is surely a question that only a man of your unique gifts and talents can satisfactorily answer. I can only try to set you upon a path that may lead you to the truth. It is a path that is strewn with danger and, as your friend in Rome has found out to his cost, one that poses a threat to life that cannot be taken too lightly.'

Holmes suddenly sat bolt upright and lit a cigarette.

'Even without the Gospel of Mary there are reasons to suppose that Peter's claims to be the natural successor to Christ are invalid and without foundation. For example, why would Jesus have chosen for a successor a man who "denied him three times" following his arrest, just as he had predicted?

'Even during the early days of the Church there was much dissention amongst the leaders as to the identity of the mysterious "disciple whom Jesus loved". The Gospel of John states that no one, not even Peter, knew Jesus as well as this enigmatic Apostle, although scholars have always assumed that this was in reference to John himself.

'Imagine, therefore, the furore that would ensue should the identity of this disciple be revealed as Mary Magdalene! This, a woman whom theological history has always erroneously condemned as being nothing more than a liberated prostitute, with no more right to lead the early Christian Church than you or I.'

I let out a long low whistle as I contemplated the enormity of Shenouda's dramatic revelation, but I soon realized that he had barely scratched the surface.

'The authority for Peter's leadership is further brought into question by the assertion that it was Mary who was the first amongst them to see a vision of the risen Christ and not Peter. She was the last at the cross and the first at the tomb! She was the one who received the instruction "Go tell Peter" from Jesus himself and she even goes on to tell Peter, "What is hidden from you, I will tell you," in reference to those teachings that Jesus deliberately withheld from him.'

With each sentence Shenouda's speech became progressively more erratic and breathless. It was almost as if in recounting the contents of the Gospel to us, he understood their true meaning for the first time and now wished to conclude our small assembly as soon as he was able.

'Are we to understand that all of these potentially damaging assertions are contained within the pages of the missing Gospel?' I asked, although fearing that I already knew the answer. Shenouda nodded his head solemnly and deliberately.

'Oh, Doctor Watson, there is still so much more to recount, yet I feel that my time is becoming as limited as your own. I will, however, make three final and vital points that will convince you of the perilous ground on which we are all now standing.

'Some of the teachings, which Jesus conveys to Mary alone, are at such variance to those within the accepted Gospels that Peter and Andrew steadfastly refused to follow the instructions of Jesus and spread his message throughout the Roman Empire. For example, he conveys the passage of the soul after death in a manner that brings to mind the bardos of *The Tibetan Book of the Dead*. It is only after Mary rebukes them both that they have a change of heart and begin their teachings.'

'It almost sounds as if Mary assumed the mantle of the leader of the Apostles, thereby bringing into question the entire male dominated ideology of the modern Church,' I commented quietly, in awe of the enormity of these revelations.

'You are quite correct, Doctor Watson, and indeed, even Mary's genealogy confirms her right to lead. In the same way as Jesus's can be traced back to King David, so Mary's goes back even further and along a far more sacred line, the

Patriarch Jacob's son Benjamin!

'You must see now, gentlemen, that the validity of this Gospel is not as crucial as is its very existence and the motives behind its theft. Now, I have detained you for far too long.'

With a sprightliness that belied his years, Shenouda leapt to his feet in a single movement and led us back along the shores of the Nile to the birthplace of our quest, the Hanging Church, otherwise known as the Church of St Mary.

'It has always been assumed that the church was named after the Mother Mary, but in the light of the contents of the Gospel, well, who can say?' Shenouda shrugged speculatively and continued to lead us at an ever-gathering pace.

By the time we arrived back within the cool interior of the church, we were all breathless and perspiring profusely. We collapsed into the coolest corner of the building and Shenouda brought us wine and refreshments. Once these had been gratefully and ravenously consumed, Shenouda stood up and clapped his hands three times and with such force that the sound echoed throughout the entire building.

An instant later, and to our great surprise, the gigantic Bedouin who had ransacked our rooms in Baker Street so many weeks ago suddenly appeared before us with his hands placed aggressively on his hips. I lost no time in drawing out my revolver and I raised its barrel towards the Bedouin's head.

'No, Doctor Watson!' Shenouda placed his hand upon the hilt of my gun and pushed it out of harm's way with surprising force.

I explained the reason behind my act of aggression and Shenouda shook his head sadly.

'It did not ever occur to you that his had been a friendly warning? We knew of the danger that you would be placing yourselves in should you have decided to take the case and we wished to prevent this. Admittedly his methods were somewhat aggressive and dramatic, but his motives were good and those methods will now stand you in good stead as he attempts to guide you safely from Egypt as I have instructed him to. Therefore, allow me to introduce you to Akhom, "The Eagle",' Shenouda announced with a broad smile.

We both bowed towards the amiable priest in gratitude and I could see that Holmes was surprisingly moved by Shenouda's gesture. In the short time that we had known him, Shenouda had made a profound impression upon us both and it was rare indeed to find Holmes so affected by another human being.

'Under the treacherous circumstances within which we all now find ourselves, I cannot, in all good conscience, accept your generous offer and thereby deny you of your own source of safety and protection.' I was proud of the honourable stance that Holmes was taking in this matter.

'Mr Holmes, now that Mary's Gospel has been removed, I am sure that I can no longer pose any real threat to the unholy trinity. So why should they waste any of their time and energy on a harmless old man?' Shenouda asked with a profound irony.

Holmes and I turned on him with raised eyebrows.

'Before you enquire into my meaning, I should remind you that haste is of the essence and you will have time enough to work out the nature of this trinity during the course of your long journey back to Rome.' Shenouda ushered us towards the exit before we could ask him another question.

'That would be the case were we journeying to Rome,' Holmes stated enigmatically.

'Where to then?' I asked, now in a state of total perplexity.

'Where else but to the town of Akhmim,' Holmes replied as if he were stating the obvious.

'Of course, I should have realized,' I mumbled sarcastically under my breath.

Holmes was not slow in recognizing my tone and so explained, with a pained expression, that an interview with Hashmoukh could prove to be of enormous value.

'Besides,' he continued, 'once we reach Cairo, a wire to Rome will soon establish whether there is any change in Gialli's condition or even some progression in the case.'

By now Akhom had gathered his things together and joined us at the top of the long staircase.

'Farewell, Mr Sherlock Holmes and Doctor Watson.'

Holmes shook the priest warmly by the hand as he encouraged us to commence our journey.

'Your help and advice has been invaluable to me,' Holmes admitted as we reluctantly took our leave. I say reluctantly because Holmes and I shared the same misgivings regarding the safety of Shenouda now that he was to be totally alone.

It was several weeks later, when we were safely ensconced within our rooms in Baker Street once more, that we received a most lamentable communication from Elraji. Shenouda had been killed within forty-eight hours of our departure. His throat had been slit open by a large curved blade!

CHAPTER ELEVEN

OUR FLIGHT FROM EGYPT

SHENOUDA WAS AS good as his word and Akhom dogged our every step throughout the journey back to Cairo.

Upon our arrival Holmes decided that we should rest up for a day or two while we awaited the replies to a number of wires that he despatched from our hotel. The reason for his wires to Rome and to Elraji I could well understand, but the motives behind the wire to his brother Mycroft were, as yet, a little less clear to me.

It was a little disconcerting to find Akhom sitting in the corridor outside of my hotel room when I awoke the following morning, although of course it was comforting in one sense. It had occurred to me that the two Bedouin, who had threatened our every step since our arrival in Alexandria, were now nowhere to be seen, and I attributed their continued absence to the presence of the gigantic Copt.

I mentioned this fact to Holmes over our breakfast and I speculated as to their motives.

'Could they be connected in some way to the unholy trinity that Shenouda made the brief reference to? Have you formulated a theory as to their identity?'

Holmes waved my questions away with a lit cigarette whose smoke drifted aimlessly over the rim of his empty coffee cup.

'Can you not save your incessant questioning until we have reached a more civilized hour of the day?' he asked petulantly. I knew that he had been harbouring certain misgivings about leaving Shenouda without his protection and in all probability had slept very little as a consequence. Furthermore, we were still awaiting the replies to his wires, so I was not entirely surprised at his tetchiness.

Nevertheless, I persisted with my enquiries once I was reasonably confident that the hour was 'more civilized'.

'Holmes,' I began tentatively, 'I must confess to being considerably more confused as a result of our consultation with Shenouda than I was before we ever met him. For example, I was convinced that our guardian, Akhom, was surely the murderer of Cardinal Tosca and yet his presence here proves that to be an impossibility.'

I was hoping that by admitting to my own failings I might appeal to Holmes's inherent desire to confirm his own authority in these matters, thereby inducing him to produce a constructive reply. Gladly, I was not to be disappointed.

We were taking shelter from the sun beneath a large canopy at the front of our hotel, while Akhom maintained an ever-watchful eye over us from the shadows. Holmes smiled towards me with a knowing intent as he slowly lit a cigarette.

'As you are without doubt aware, Watson, I am loath to impart any theories which I might be harbouring until I am absolutely certain of my facts. On this occasion I must confess to not having been entirely honest with you from the outset nor in my diagnosis of the case thus far. As a matter of fact, I was not entirely convinced of Akhom's involvement in Tosca's murder from the moment that I began my examination of his office window.'

I was not totally surprised about receiving this type of confession from Holmes, for I had heard so many of a similar nature from him during the course of our previous cases. I was certain that my disgruntled demeanour gave away something of how I was feeling about this latest one, when Holmes hurriedly continued, giving me little time to express my indignation.

'You must understand, Watson, that it is the one vital piece of evidence that pointed accusingly in Akhom's direction, or at least away from that of the true guilty party, that is also the one that has now exonerated him in my eyes. I am referring, of course, to the shape of the blade that was used in both the slaying of Cardinal Tosca and in the prising open of his office window.'

'In heaven's name, Holmes!' I exclaimed in a state of some exasperation. 'I could see for myself that the curvature of the blade is identical to the one used so ably by Akhom in Baker Street.'

'Of course it is, Watson, and assuredly by design. However, there is one singular aspect that has undoubtedly gone unnoticed by yourself, Inspector Gialli and the Vatican authorities. A trained observer would have noted that the blade mark upon the window frame indicated that the window had in actual fact been forced open from the inside!'

'From the inside!' I repeated excitedly.

'There is no doubt of it, in my view. Obviously the implications of this fact alone are very clear, are they not, Watson?' Holmes sank back into his chair as if he were inviting me to expand my own view of the matter.

'Indeed they are, for not only are Akhom and other members of his creed absolved of all guilt but there are now strong grounds to suppose that the murderer of Cardinal Tosca was trying his very best to implicate members of that very same group. I am, of course, referring to the Orthodox

Coptic Church.'

Holmes clapped his hands together gleefully and leant forward once again.

'Oh, this is inspired work, Watson! Clearly the early-morning Egyptian air has gone some way towards reawakening your naturally dormant mental powers.' Despite my natural inclination towards rage, I could not help but smile at Holmes's misguided attempt at bestowing praise.

'A fine compliment indeed!' I chided him with an expression of exaggerated annoyance.

'Watson, you must excuse my inept attempts at humour, for you have assuredly acquired a full understanding of how things really stand. Now that we are armed with this knowledge, the undertones have attained a far darker hue.'

'Who then would undertake such a ghastly venture and why would they possibly wish to implicate the Copts?' I asked.

'Watson, surely the enlightening time that we were able to spend in the company of the brilliant Shenouda has gone some way towards resolving the second part of your question. I can see no good reason to doubt Shenouda's interpretation of the Gospel of Mary, so therefore the motive for the crime becomes self-evident, namely the suppression of that Gospel! As to the identity of the criminal, well, I have to tell you that to date I have only been able to formulate four separate theories.' Holmes made this outrageous statement without a trace of humour, either in his voice or upon his face.

'Only four, Holmes? You do surprise me!' I responded sarcastically.

Holmes cast me a brief, cursory glance before he continued.

'Before I can test each one of these, it is absolutely essential that I interview the man who has initiated this entire circle of events: the thief Hashmoukh.'

'That explains your urgent desire to visit the town of

Akhmim, rather than making a hasty return to Rome.' I vocalized my mental confirmation in hushed tones, which Holmes either did not hear or chose to ignore.

'Upon our arrival in Akhmim we shall be met by Elraji, who is certain that he will have Hashmoukh safely in detention by the time that we three meet.

'So, would you go, Watson, to the waterfront, in the company of the resolute Akhom, and endeavour to locate and engage a felucca for our journey. Obviously, if you can find your Nubian, then so much the better, for he is surely a far better boatman than my captain could ever hope to be.'

I rose from my chair without a moment's hesitation, and from the corner of my eye I could see that Akhom was prepared to follow my every step. Naturally I had certain misgivings about leaving Holmes so isolated in the midst of such potential dangers. Holmes identified this dilemma, upon my face, at once. He smiled sympathetically.

'Do not concern yourself unduly, Doctor, for I am about to retire to the cool of the hotel lobby. There I shall be perfectly safe under the watchful eye of the commissioner and his cohorts. By the time that I have consumed a copious amount of Turkish coffee and a shisha or two, you will have returned to find me safe and well. Good luck and farewell!'

I could not offer a single, significant word of protest to Holmes's pronouncement and soon, with Akhom securely in tow, I found myself once more down upon the jetty.

My search had been barely five minutes old when, by a strange quirk of fate – or had it been a miracle, for by now I was prepared to believe almost anything – I found the insightful Nubian.

In all honesty it would be more accurate to state that he found me. His huge booming voice could be heard around the length and breadth of the entire jetty as soon as he saw me arrive.

He leapt up from his boat and onto the jetty in an instant and although he eyed Akhom with some suspicion initially, he greeted me warmly, if a little painfully. He laughed aloud when he saw me nursing my shoulder.

'So, Englishman, I see that you wish to engage my humble vessel once again. No doubt for the journey that you intend to make to Akhmim with your friends!' He made this startling statement without even the faintest quiver of doubt in his voice.

'How can you possibly know that?' I asked in amazement, and again the jetty reverberated with the depth of the Nubian's laughter.

'Oh, that is an easy question to answer, Englishman. Your friend Elraji has gone on ahead of you and he asked me to keep an eye out for you.' Then he lowered his voice and took me to one side. 'You should be aware, however, that the journey that we are about to undertake is a far different proposition to the one that we have made upriver previously. We shall be traversing some of the narrower stretches of the river where our progress will depend more upon the currents and nuances of the river than upon my own great skills.' He made this last statement with neither a trace of humour or arrogance in his voice. 'We have over two hundred miles to cover, so if you intend to arrive in Akhmim before nightfall, we must depart within the hour!' he announced.

I did not need to be told twice. I nodded my head in an emphatic acceptance of this plan and while I scrambled back up and away from the jetty, I could hear the Nubian clap his hands resoundingly as he galvanized his crew into readying his vessel with all speed.

The urgency of our situation was clear to me and so Akhom and I literally sprinted for the entire length of our journey back to the hotel. Therefore, my consternation at finding the lobby empty can be well understood. I extended my search for

Holmes to his bedroom and then to the dining room; however, each time I was met by the same lack of success.

In my desperation I beseeched every member of staff that I encountered for news of Holmes's current location, only to be met by the slow, solemn shaking of their heads. I sank down upon my haunches on the steps that led up to the hotel entrance, with my head cupped within my hands. I was trying to search for an explanation for Holmes's mysterious disappearance when I heard a familiar and surprisingly cheerful voice call out to me.

'My dear fellow, you really should know better than to run around in such excessive heat!'

I could not contain my anger for a moment longer.

'I was under the impression that our departure for Akhmim was a matter of some urgency! Besides, you assured me that you were to remain within the relative safety of the hotel lobby. How was I to know what had become of you?'

'I can assure you, Watson, that it was nothing more sinister than an invitation to a local shisha lounge where they serve a very pleasant, if not heady, blend of hashish. You should try some, Watson; it is a most illuminating experience, I assure you.'

I could see from his eyes that Holmes's experience had been somewhat more than a little illuminating!

'I simply cannot understand how a man of your refined intellect could repeatedly jeopardize the state of his physical and mental well-being with these flagrant, intoxicating abuses. Surely the situation of our current case is supplying you with more than a sufficient amount of stimulation?' I suggested with not a little anger and frustration in my voice.

I could see that, even in his current condition, Holmes was able to appreciate the intention behind my scolding. His face suddenly dropped, as did his voice.

'Watson, I must thank you, once again, for your persistent

attempts at inducing in me a sense of self-preservation. You are quite correct to admonish my behaviour which is, under our present set of circumstances, more than a little reprehensible. Now, I can see from the condition of your clothing that you have been able to locate your Nubian and that he advises an immediate departure. We must grab a few things and make for the docks immediately!' he pronounced with an alacrity that belied his state of intoxication.

We left the majority of our luggage in our rooms and I found myself speeding towards the jetty once more. As it transpired, we arrived at the boat with barely a few moments to spare. My Nubian friend was standing upon his hand rail waving his arms frantically above his head.

'Hurry, my friends!' he called out urgently. 'In but a moment or two the tide will be against us.'

We leapt upon the deck as a crewman began to untie the ropes, but I noticed that Holmes took an awkward tumble as he landed next to me. A moment later we began the journey to Akhmim.

Akhom assumed a seated position, high upon the stern of the felucca, which afforded him a view of all aboard the boat. There he remained throughout the entire journey, his face immovable and inscrutable, his huge arms crossed upon his waist with one hand resting upon the hilt of his sword, almost resembling a converse figure head.

By way of a contrast, Holmes lay stretched out upon his back, with his eyes shut tight beneath the rim of his hat. He would barely move from this position until the journey was almost completed and once the poison within him had almost exhausted itself.

Left to my own devices, I found it fascinating to observe the varied and spectacular landscapes which lined each bank, as our vessel slid by them with a swift but silent momentum. I was smoking thoughtfully upon my pipe when the Nubian decided to take a seat next to mine as he lit up a small reed pipe of his own.

'You are fascinated by these strange and ancient lands, are you not, Doctor Watson?' I glanced across at him in surprise for a moment. 'It was not hard for me to realize that the good doctor would accompany Sherlock Holmes upon his journeys.' We smiled at each other and he offered me his hand, which I accepted warmly.

'My name is Taharka,' he announced with an air of some importance. Then he smiled. 'Do not be alarmed, Doctor Watson, for I have no illusions as to my station. My parents obviously believed me to be destined for greater things, as they named me after one of the greatest Nubian rulers to have ever lived.

'Taharka was not only a ruler over the Nubians but he was also a King of Egypt known as the ruler of the two lands.' Then he pointed down to a large ornate buckle that clasped together his belt and which was in the shape of twin cobra heads. 'The two cobras signify the two lands that my namesake ruled over all those years ago.'

Taharka then fell into a protracted and melancholy silence, as he no doubt reflected upon the tricks of fate that shape our destinies. He then launched into a fascinating historical summary of the ancient city that we were rapidly being drawn towards.

Akhmim was a city whose origins can be traced back to a period of over 6,000 years ago when it was a centre of worship for followers of a variety of Egyptian deities including the 'God King' Rameses II. Later on it became an important textile town, known during the Greco-Roman era as Panapolis.

Rather interestingly in the light of our current quest, during the Christian era, when it was known as Shmin, a large number of Christian Copts gathered in the area, including a famous fourth-century monk known as Shenouda of

Archimandrite, who died under mysterious circumstances that never came to light.

I was disappointed to learn that the vast majority of the ancient buildings and monuments, which had a fabled beauty and magnificence, had been pulled apart and pillaged by the occupants of the late Middle Ages. Those bricks and dismantled monoliths were subsequently used in the construction of Coptic churches and many of the civic buildings that still stand today.

Apparently many of these Churches revealed ancient Christian writings that were every bit as interesting and potentially as controversial as the Gospel of Mary Magdalene. Small wonder, therefore, that Hashmoukh saw fit to ply his scurrilous trade within those ancient and derelict walls.

By the time that Taharka had completed his historical monologue, I noticed that Holmes had begun to emerge from his unnatural slumber. With a loud groan he allowed the sun to beat down upon his forehead from under the rim of his hat and he began to rub his already reddened eyes with the palms of his hands. He propped himself up on an elbow and smiled towards Taharka and I as he lit a cigarette.

'Ah, Watson, I can see, from the position of the sun, that we have made good progress during the course of my incapacitation!' he called out hoarsely. Taharka immediately threw a gourd of water across to him and Holmes drank from this, greedily and thankfully.

'Do not reproach me again, Doctor, for I assure you that, on this occasion, I have learnt my lesson.' Holmes clearly anticipated what would have been my next sentence.

'Well, I am certainly glad to hear that!' I confirmed emphatically.

Holmes slowly made his way back up onto his feet and Taharka came over to point out the distant and shimmering visions that were the outer suburbs of Akhmim slowly coming into view. I gave Holmes a brief outline of Taharka's historical summary, so that he would have had some idea of what to expect upon our arrival, and he appeared to have been surprisingly interested.

As our boat moved ever closer to our objective, a familiar figure slowly came into focus upon the diminishing horizon. We were all glad to see that Elraji was still safe and well and ready to greet us. Yet, as his features gradually clarified, we could see from the furrowed brow and his haunted eyes that all was not well.

Then, as we prepared to disembark, Holmes suddenly turned towards Taharka in a state of great agitation.

'Please be prepared to make the return journey within the hour. If the look upon the face of Elraji is anything to go by, I would say that our interview with Hashmoukh will prove to be a lot briefer than I had originally hoped for.' Holmes issued this instruction with more than a little bitterness in his voice and I was shocked at the harshness of the tone that Holmes had used when addressing Taharka. However, in retrospect, I should not have been that surprised.

As Elraji held out his hands, to help us both climb up and on to the jetty, our worst fears were immediately confirmed. I received the briefest of acknowledgements as Elraji began to express his regrets to Holmes in the most demonstrative of fashions.

'Oh, Mr Holmes, I must offer you at least a thousand apologies! Undoubtedly we have arrived too late ... too late. I have wasted your time and your efforts in making this long journey. Hashmoukh is already dead!'

Holmes did not appear to have been altogether surprised when he heard this news and I am certain that he regretted the loss of a vital clue far more than he felt for the loss of another human life. For Holmes the work was everything and the death of Hashmoukh was nothing more than another stumbling block that obstructed his pathway to the truth.

'Have you taken all precautions?' Holmes asked of me and I patted the jacket pocket that held my revolver, by way of a confirmation. Holmes nodded to Elraji.

'You may now show us the way.'

Without another word, Elraji slowly led us away from the river and towards a derelict bazaar that surrounded a motley collection of unremarkable and badly run-down shops. He made directly towards a small textile business on the far corner of the thoroughfare and as we reached its colourfully decorated front, Elraji immediately ducked down a dark alleyway that led to the rear of the shop.

This alley was totally cut off from any kind of fresh and moving air by two sandstone walls and a large canopy of soiled cotton. As a consequence, the stench that greeted us and soon enveloped us was almost indescribable. We picked our way gingerly through a morass of every conceivable type of flotsam and finally began a short ascent to a tiny room at the head of a flight of wooden steps.

This, the living quarters and the final resting place of Hashmoukh the manuscript thief, was by far the vilest example of squalor that either of us had ever previously encountered. Every surface was liberally caked in every conceivable shade of brown that one could imagine. This extended even to the curtains and the bed linen, which was now also stained in blood.

We all placed handkerchiefs over our noses and mouths, in our efforts at masking the all-pervading toxic vapours, but in vain. We moved towards the body, but only to a distance that we dare not pass. Hashmoukh had clearly been upon his bed when the assassin struck, for the pool of blood was far larger and deeper in shade than where his body now lay.

However, death had obviously not been instantaneous, because the odious little man had subsequently dragged himself along the floor to a distance no less than four feet away from where the assassin had struck. He had finally expired on a small straw mat in the middle of the room. Hashmoukh had ended up flat on his back and his emaciated face was lying directly below a slow-moving fan that was achieving nothing more than the circulation of the steamy, noxious air and a swarm of flies that had begun to feast upon his skin. His eyes were red and raw and, like the rest of his face, they were masked with the fear of his impending doom.

To my dismay, Holmes suddenly removed his handkerchief. He crouched down onto the floor and invited me to join him there. Against my better judgement, I immediately followed his lead and then proceeded to examine the gaping wound that had been scored across the dead man's neck. I was able to confirm at once that the cause of death was a weapon identical to the one that had ended the life of Cardinal Tosca!

I was relieved that my examination had proved to be such a brief one, for I was not sure if I would have been able to hold my breath for too much longer. I replaced my handkerchief at the first opportunity but I regarded Holmes's flagrant disregard of his own well-being with a mixture of both admiration and stark horror, as he remained on the floor with his face uncovered.

Holmes followed the trail of blood that Hashmoukh had left behind him as he had clambered from his bed. Clearly he had begun his last, painful journey on his knees, but his strength soon gave out and he rolled over for the last time. Holmes tried to understand the reason behind Hashmoukh's final and titanic effort by following the direction of his blank, starting eyes, but this revealed nothing.

'Doctor, how long after the attack would you estimate that death might have occurred?' Holmes asked me suddenly.

'Ordinarily a pair of severed carotid arteries will result in an instantaneous death. So that means that Hashmoukh must have moved with some speed and no little determination to have gained as much ground as he did before he finally expired,' I replied.

Holmes acknowledged this information with a sharp nod of his head, before he turned his attention to Elraji.

'Inspector, can you state with any certainty the time at which the body was first discovered?'

'I was called to the scene of the crime some four hours before I met you at the boat. However, the old lady who operates the shop below Hashmoukh's lodgings states that she heard what seemed to be a struggle taking place in the room above her. This commotion occurred at least six hours before the alarm was finally raised.'

'Why was there such a long period between the two events?' Holmes asked in disbelief.

'The old lady was alarmed by the sounds of violence and was understandably nervous of venturing upstairs until such time as her nephew had returned from making his deliveries. It was this young man who eventually discovered the body and sent for the police,' Elraji confirmed.

Holmes now fell into an introspective silence and he barely acknowledged Elraji's concise reply. He climbed back slowly onto his feet and meticulously cast his gaze around the room before he spoke next.

'So, it is quite conceivable that rigor mortis has already set in?' Holmes asked of both Elraji and me.

We both nodded our affirmation.

'Even in this heat, I would say that after ten hours it is more than likely,' I confirmed, although I could not understand, as yet, the reason behind Holmes's current line of questioning.

As if sensing my confusion, Holmes suddenly emitted a grunt of impatience and frustration.

'His hand, Watson, look at his hand! Rigor mortis has mummified his right hand as if it were in the process of trying to grasp something. Our task is to try to understand the nature of the object that he considered to be so important at the last.'

Sure enough, the fingers of Hashmoukh's right hand had remained tightly bent as if he was trying to grip a very small object indeed. I groaned silently once I realized that this discovery of Holmes would delay still further our return to the relatively fresher air outside.

In this I was proved to be correct. Holmes insisted on examining every inch of the room that lay within the scope of Hashmoukh's final eye line. Finally Holmes's gaze rested upon a small bamboo table, which was propped up upon a pile books, in the far corner of the room.

I almost recoiled in horror as I began to recognize the original form of some of the congealing and decomposing forms that lay upon the surface of the table. I found it almost impossible to watch Holmes as his long, dextrous fingers flittered gingerly between each of these objects as he searched for the one thing that Hashmoukh seemed to value above all others.

When Holmes did finally manage to make his discovery it was in a manner that proved to be far less dramatic than I might have anticipated. He merely slipped a small buff envelope out of his inside pocket and placed within it a small piece of battered card that had lost all four of its corners and had been sitting on the middle of the table beneath a pile of fish bones.

I watched Holmes as he brushed himself down and I could see that he bore a look of satisfaction that both confused me and infused me with fresh hope and optimism.

'Despite the poisonous and potentially lethal properties of the atmosphere in which we have had to operate, I have to admit that this has proven to be a most satisfying afternoon's work, if not a conclusive one!' Holmes jovially announced as he led the way back down the stairs to the street once more.

'One that I hope justifies the enormous risk that you have subjected us all to?' I ventured, once we all felt that we could breathe freely once more.

Holmes lit a cigarette as he pondered the motive behind my last question.

'In this case, at least, the end certainly justifies the means,' Holmes answered quietly and as inscrutably as usual. I was resolved to discovering the nature of the contents of that envelope at some future date.

'Now, we must execute our departure from these majestic yet troubled lands, with all the speed that is available to us!' Holmes indicated, with a sweep of his arm, that we should follow him back towards the pier. Only Elraji stood firm and he shook his head apologetically once Holmes realized that he would not be joining us upon the return journey.

'Oh, Mr Holmes, I am afraid that I must remain here to help clear up the mess upstairs and then make my report. If I receive any further information, I will forward it to your brother in London. Besides, you are already travelling with good and able companions.' Elraji pointed to Akhom and I with a short, sharp salute and he clicked his heels as he turned smartly.

Once again I found myself sprinting towards Taharka's boat and a short while later we found ourselves gliding effortlessly towards Cairo for the last time.

When I say 'effortlessly' I am, of course, referring to the labour required of the passengers that were aboard, namely Akhom, Holmes and myself. However, the inward journey to Cairo was proving to be a far more trying affair for Taharka and his crew as had been the outward.

Taharka had insisted that we depart from Cairo with all speed, so that we might find the tides and currents favourable to our intent. Now, however, we were discovering that these same elements were having the opposite effect. As a consequence, in order to minimize these counter currents, Taharka was constantly altering the position of his sail, while his crewmen were not permitted to leave the rudder unattended even for an instant.

The fact that they were working in the dark acted as a further impediment and there was little doubt that Taharka and I would not be engaging in any further discussions on this particular voyage. I decided to put my head down upon the deck, as I was sure that this would prove to be a very long night.

Just before I pulled my hat down over my eyes, I noticed that Holmes was seated upright at the bow with his pipe perpetually billowing out its familiar, dark grey smoke into the fresh night air. It was almost as if he were imagining that his efforts were in some way propelling the felucca to ever greater speeds and hastening our urgent return to Rome.

In this he was to be sadly mistaken and the return journey to Cairo proved to be almost twice the length of the voyage to Akhmim! As we left the boat, Holmes barely acknowledged the efforts made by Taharka and his crew, on our behalf, so intent was he on planning the next stage of our journey and despatching wires from our hotel.

On the other hand, I felt a certain pride at having made the acquaintance of the giant Nubian and accepted the fact that our paths would never cross again with a sad resignation. We clasped hands as we made our farewells.

'May the remainder of your quest be favoured with good fortune and fair winds, Englishman!' Taharka said this with the fervour of a prayer.

'God's speed, oh ruler of the two lands!' I responded with equal sincerity. As Akhom and I turned towards the hotel, Taharka was already barking orders at his young crewman.

I arrived in the lobby just as Holmes was despatching his two wires and then, to my great surprise, he proposed an early lunch. We sat down to a plateful of melon, goat's cheese and olives and I was amazed at the enthusiasm Holmes displayed as he devoured it. I sat back and observed him with some amusement.

'By employing your method, Holmes, I deduce that you have discovered far more, within Hashmoukh's room, than either Elraji or I ever could.'

Holmes smiled at me condescendingly as he wiped his mouth with a napkin.

'You have based this deduction purely upon the fact that I have cleared my plate of food?' Holmes asked me as he slowly lit a cigarette. I reluctantly nodded my affirmation as I lit one of my own.

'Did it not occur to you that perhaps I did so simply because I was hungry? I have often felt obliged to explain to you, in your capacity as my doctor, that I have regularly abstained from any sustenance during the course of a case, as I cannot afford the enormous expenditure of energy that is involved in the digestion of food.

'Although I am clearly involved in what is undoubtedly the greatest challenge of my career to date, I am also aware of the fact that for the next few days, at least, I will be engaged in doing nothing more energetic than sitting idly by while a succession of trains and boats slowly bring me towards my desired destination. You may be assured that there will be further empty plates before we finally reach the gates of Rome!' Holmes concluded.

'Oh, but Holmes, you cannot deny that you bore an air of self-satisfaction as we finally left the hell that had been Hashmoukh's room. Surely that has gone some way towards explaining your newfound appetite?' I insisted.

Holmes eyed me quizzically through a plume of smoke before he finally relented.

'As you are so certain of the results of your instinctive

reasoning, I will not deny it. However, before you question me further, be aware that I will disclose nothing more until I have put everything to the test upon our return to Rome.'

'Could you at least inform me of the names of the intended recipients of the two wires that you have despatched with such urgency?'

'Surely they must be self-evident, even to you? Obviously one is on its way to our friend Inspector Gialli in Rome. I am certain that by now he is fully recovered and able to assist me once more with my inquiries. The other will hopefully find its way to my brother Mycroft. I expect to receive a reply to both before our train to Alexandria departs tomorrow afternoon.'

Holmes refused to be drawn any further upon the matter at hand and we spent a fascinating afternoon and evening amongst the sights and sounds of the bazaar. As the sun slowly sank below the horizon, a thousand torches and fires suddenly sprang into life upon every stall and at each corner of the bazaar.

The exciting sights, sounds and smells all seemed to intensify as the darkness gradually descended and the milieu became more and more feverish with each passing moment. Holmes and I managed to find a quieter enclave on the fringes of the activity, where we were able to take a cup of coffee and a surprisingly good Cognac. As we concluded our final pipes of the day, we slowly left the table and began to make our way back to the hotel. It was then that I saw them.

At first I did not point them out to Holmes, because in the midst of the surrounding turmoil I could not be certain of the accuracy of my observation. However, as we neared the hotel and the density of the crowds gradually began to thin, there was surely no mistaking them. The two Bedouins, who had shadowed our every step from the outset of our journey, were behind us once more! This was no discreet attempt at surveillance, for this time there was a more determined and menacing intent behind their movements.

It was at this point I decided to alert Holmes and he encouraged me to duck into the front doorway of a carpet shop, once we had turned the nearest corner. I pulled out my revolver and we were resolved to remaining there until our would-be assailants passed our vantage point and we could then gain the higher ground.

They had only been a few yards behind us before we had turned the corner, so we had estimated that they would have been upon us almost immediately if they had continued at their previous speed. However, as the minutes ticked away, we soon came to realize that the Bedouins had inexplicably changed their plans or directions. My hand began to perspire upon the handle of my gun and I turned to Holmes for guidance.

Holmes was staring out into the night sky with a steely intensity that made his hawk-like features appear to be almost rigid and statuesque. In this quarter of the town, at least, the excitement of the evening had suddenly been doused and an all-pervading silence had descended upon these tiny back streets.

It had become obvious, after five minutes or more had passed, that the Bedouins were no longer following in our footsteps and we slowly edged out from our recess, although Holmes did indicate that I should remain armed until he was certain that the danger no longer existed. An extended search of each of the surrounding streets soon confirmed that this was so and we made our way slowly but anxiously back to our hotel.

The sudden disappearance of the two Bedouins should really have come as no great surprise to us, in retrospect. Earlier in the day Akhom had begged our leave that he might visit his aged and ailing mother who resided within the

Coptic quarter of the city.

Naturally enough we had granted his request without a moment's hesitation, but we were now glad to see that his return had been so well timed. Sure enough, the Bedouins had made their retreat from the very moment that Akhom had resumed his duties and Holmes and I could now rest easy knowing that we were, once again, under the ever-watchful eye of Shenouda's servant.

We spent the following morning anxiously awaiting the arrival of the replies to Holmes's wires. There was little or no chance of them ever catching up with us should they have arrived after our departure. Equally the urgency of our return to Rome precluded us from spurning a berth aboard the first available train to leave for Alexandria, which was scheduled to depart almost immediately after lunch.

Our packing was done and all of our preparations were in hand. I took breakfast alone and then found Holmes pacing up and down incessantly upon the forecourt outside of the hotel's main entrance. I could see from the piles of tobacco ash that marked out his boundaries that he attached a good deal more importance to those impending replies than I could have possibly imagined.

To my great relief, the wires arrived within minutes of each other and a full thirty minutes before we were due to leave our hotel. To my dismay, however, Holmes did not appear to be so relieved upon reading their contents. He rolled each one into a tight ball and ensured that I should not unravel them by hurling them into a passing dust cart.

'Even upon such an adventure and in such distant and exotic lands, you seem to be intent upon keeping me in ignorance once more,' I complained.

'I can assure you, Watson, that there is nothing within those scraps of paper that would serve to enlighten you any further. My obvious frustration is not born of the contents of those wires, but of what they do not contain. I have to tell you that, once again, you and I are destined to play a dangerous double-handed game and I curse the day that I involved you in such an enterprise,' Holmes said with a great intensity.

'I am sorry that you consider my company and contribution of such little value,' I said, unable to conceal my hurt.

'Oh, my dear fellow, I assure you that the truth is the exact opposite and I would never underestimate your abilities. However, I sincerely hope that by involving you I have not put your life in jeopardy.'

'I would not have it any other way, old fellow. Besides, we have been in many a tight scrape in the past, have we not?'

'Of course we have, Watson.' Holmes slapped me upon my shoulder; however, I could tell from his tone that he was not entirely convinced by his own reassurances.

There was something unsettling in Holmes's manner from the moment that he had received those replies and as we made our way towards the station I found myself constantly glancing over my shoulder, despite the presence of Akhom.

My misgivings soon proved to have some foundation, for, as we stepped out upon the platform, two very familiar figures appeared menacingly at the opposite end. They were walking towards us with urgency and intent. The train was now ready for an immediate departure and we hurriedly handed our baggage over to a porter, who then guided us to our carriage.

At that moment, before we were able to climb aboard, both Bedouins suddenly pulled out revolvers and immediately opened fire upon us! Twice, or perhaps three times, we heard the sounds of ricochet as their bullets narrowly failed to find their mark and I pulled out my own revolver to return their fire. The accuracy of their gunfire was barring our way onto the train and a moment later we heard the guard blow his final whistle.

Yet, just as we were despairing of ever managing to board the train – indeed it had already begun to make a steady progress away from the platform – Akhom suddenly sprang between the Bedouins and ourselves with his sword swirling menacingly above his head.

Our assailants were so taken aback by this sudden assault that neither of them was able to let off a single clear shot before Akhom's sword began to find its mark. His immediate targets were the hands that held the revolvers. His strikes and the blade itself were so true that each hand was dismembered by a single blow.

His second swings cleaved a wide and deadly gash across each of their chests and as we finally swung ourselves aboard the train we could see that both Bedouins had been duly despatched. We looked back, as the train finally cleared the platform, to see Akhom holding his sword aloft and above his head in a display of triumph. He then bade us farewell with a loud roar that almost drowned out the sound of our train as it began to gain momentum.

'The poor fellow has sacrificed much in ensuring our safe departure,' I remarked with a sad shaking of my head.

'Not so, Watson. Upon our arrival in Alexandria, I will immediately despatch a wire to Elraji that will explain the circumstances of Akhom's deadly mayhem and guarantee his continued liberty. You see, even now he remains unharassed as he leaves the station.' Holmes pointed towards the gigantic Copt as he resheathed his sword and then began to walk slowly away from the scene of his carnage

As Cairo finally disappeared from our view, Holmes and I had good cause to reflect upon our fate had Akhom's warning to us in Baker Street not been a friendly one.

CHAPTER TWELVE

THE UNHOLY TRINITY

HOLMES WAS AS good as his word and as soon as we had arrived safely in Alexandria, he despatched the wire to Elraji that would undoubtedly ensure the liberty of Akhom.

Obviously, our next task was to secure ourselves a berth on board the next available sailing to Brindisi. This we had no great difficulty in achieving; however, the only boat that was available to us was a mail packet ship that threatened a journey considerably longer than our outward journey had been. The only alternative was to wait in Alexandria for a further three days until there was a direct sailing.

We chose the lesser of the two evils and two hours later we were stowing our luggage aboard the *Ptolemy*. Thankfully the glass was set fair, so the crossing was smooth and comfortable. Holmes soon became surprisingly resigned to the length of time that we would be spending aboard and before long we began to speculate as to the identity of the unholy trinity.

We pulled two wicker chairs closer together on the small deck and as he lit a pipe, Holmes invited me to voice my opinion.

'Do not look so surprised, Watson. As you already know,

your opinions, no matter how erroneous and ill-advised they might have been, have often proved to be of the utmost value to me on many similar occasions. Perhaps the process of dismissing these has inspired me to produce a far more logical and meritorious result.'

'Well, as long as I have been of some use....' Holmes was evidently oblivious to my sarcastic response because he continued as if there had been none.

'Watson, you have seen and heard everything that I have been privy to and therefore I would greatly appreciate your opinion as to the identity of the unholy trinity that Shenouda referred to.' Despite his previous deprecating observation, Holmes's request did appear to be a genuine one and therefore I was determined to ensure that I would make an equable contribution.

'It is an unusual phrase, as it seems to imply that there are three people connected to this case who are the exact opposite of the very cornerstone of the Christian faith. I am, of course, referring to the Father, the Son and the Holy Spirit.'

Holmes did seem to be paying full attention to my words, and his eyes didn't leave me, even while he was lighting his pipe. Therefore I decided to continue as best I could.

'As you have so emphatically pointed out, Shenouda has been of immeasurable assistance to us. Consequently, I would not be a bit surprised if, once we have isolated the nature of this trinity, we should then be able to identify not only the murderer of Cardinal Tosca but also the person, or persons, behind the theft of the missing Gospel and the attack upon Inspector Gialli!'

'Oh, this is excellent, Watson,' Holmes commented. I could tell from the intensity of his alert and hawklike features that this compliment had indeed been a sincere one.

'Furthermore, there is little doubt in my mind that one of the leading players within this drama will turn out to be Kyrillos Makarios, the Patriarch of the Coptic Catholic Church,' I continued.

'Despite Shenouda's refusal to accept the possibility of his involvement, it seems to me that he has more to gain than anyone else, should the Gospel of Mary be placed into the wrong hands. Surely if the Orthodox Church were to be accused of heresy, then it would not be long before the Patriarchy of all of Africa would fall into the hands of Makarios.' I sank back into my chair, confident that I had finally been able to make a worthwhile contribution.

Holmes stared at me in total silence for what seemed to be an eternity and I could not be sure if my statement was going to receive a positive response. Finally Holmes shook his head resoundingly and repetitively.

'No, no, no,' he said slowly and very quietly. 'All that we have heard about Cardinal Tosca seems to have indicated that he was a man of a scholastic disposition with an open mind and a passion for ancient and unusual texts. Why then would Makarios send the parchment to a man who had no intention of using it to discredit the Orthodox Church?'

I could not be sure as to whether Holmes's question had been a rhetorical one or not. In any event, I must admit to have been totally unable to offer a reasonable response to it. Perhaps he had decided to voice a question that had been nagging away inside his own head?

'I am certain that he would not. However, you cannot deny that Makarios would greatly benefit from the Gospel's contents being exposed. Besides, it seems more likely to me that our Bedouin friends, of murderous intent, would have been in Makarios' employ rather than any of the other players in this drama.' I was certain of receiving a negative response, almost from the moment those words had left my lips.

Holmes continued to stare at me with that intense silence and he seemed reluctant to dismiss my last statement without giving it due consideration.

'Watson, there is certainly an element of truth in what you say. Yet I still feel that there is one obvious factor whose significance has, so far, eluded me,' Holmes said glumly.

'You seem to be reluctant to accept my hypothesis regarding Makarios and yet you have failed to reveal any ideas of your own regarding the identities of the trinity,' I said by way of a challenge to my friend.

Holmes, on the other hand, was in no mood for such rudimentary games.

'You have given me much to dwell upon, Watson. I think that I will take a quiet turn about the deck.' There was no mistaking his desire for solitude, in both his voice and his manner, so I made no attempt at accompanying him, perhaps in anticipation of him returning with a full and final explanation.

I continued to enjoy the rarefied air while I awaited Holmes's return and before too long our first glimpse of Europe, namely the western coast of Greece at Cape Rataplan, came into view. However, as each successive port of call came and went, it became increasingly evident to me that Holmes would not be drawn any further upon the subject of the nature of the unholy trinity, at least until our return to Rome.

At any rate, this afforded me time enough for speculation of my own. Both Holmes and Shenouda had been similarly dismissive of my assertion that Makarios was involved in some way, although their reasons for doing so were still a mystery to me.

However, if this did prove to be the case, who were the members of this impious triumvirate? Of course, the murderer of Cardinal Tosca was one obvious candidate, despite the fact that his identity was still much shrouded in mystery. Until such time as this was finally revealed, I decided to consider the notion that Professor Ronald Sydney might also be a member of this trinity.

141

By all accounts he was a renowned, almost fanatical collector of ancient Christian texts. Furthermore, he was a regular customer of Hashmoukh and would have been greatly aggrieved to discover that Mary's Gospel had been sent to Cardinal Tosca instead of to himself.

Although all of the recognized facts seemed to preclude the notion that Sydney was in fact the murderer of Cardinal Tosca, there seemed to be little cause to doubt his involvement in this affair. After all, was he not an avid collector of the very kind of artefact that was stolen from Tosca's office? The fact that Gialli's assailants spoke with an English accent also seemed to point in Sydney's direction.

An expert as renowned as he was would have had little difficulty in identifying the value of a parchment as important as the Gospel of Mary Magdalene. Evidently he was prepared to go to any lengths in achieving its ownership, or even just a portion of it.

Yet how did he even know of the Gospel's presence upon Tosca's desk? Hashmoukh must have been aware of the danger he faced if ever Sydney were to discover that he had sold the scroll before offering it to him first, so he would not have told him of its existence. Sydney was certainly not collaborating with the murderer, for he had retained the portions of the scroll which he considered to be of the greatest significance for himself.

Regardless of what had been the source of this knowledge, I regarded the fact that he even had that information, daunting enough in itself. Surely that seemed to indicate that he actually had a collaborator within the walls of the Vatican!

So vital did he regard the possession of that portion that he even declared his hand openly by despatching two London thugs onto the streets of Rome and having a policeman beaten to within an inch of his life! I was now convinced that the professor must have had some very influential friends if he could afford to act with such a reckless confidence. Was it possible that one of those friends would actually prove to be the third member of the trinity?

I decided to abandon my speculation for the time being as I saw Holmes finally walk towards me with some purpose. Unfortunately, he had merely come to inform me that he had decided to take to his cabin for an hour or so and that he wished to apologize for having abandoned me to my own devices for so long. I waved this aside with aplomb, as I watched him go below decks, and I now decided to take more of an interest in our voyage.

This I had not been able to do on the outward journey, for I had devoted my entire attention to the two threatening Bedouins who had plagued our every move throughout the voyage. However, I was to be disappointed, even in this endeavour. I found the sea to be flat and featureless and our ports of call were too brief to have been of any interest.

The speed of our mail packet compensated for the fact that we were making considerably more calls as we made our way through both the Ionian and then the Adriatic seas. My conversations with an amiable young lieutenant revealed that we would be arriving in Brindisi exactly three days after our departure from Alexandria.

It would not be an exaggeration to say that, throughout that time, I exchanged more dialogue with that lieutenant than I managed to with my troubled friend. Cape Rataplan had soon come and gone and by the time that we had reached Corfu again, via the Ionian Isles and Zante, I had become most anxious for Holmes's well-being.

However, upon sighting Otranto on the heel of Italy, Holmes visibly bucked up once more and he became excited at the prospect of finally concluding the case upon our return to Rome. Exactly how he proposed to do this was something that he was still reluctant to reveal to me, but his positive demeanour imbued me with renewed optimism.

By the time we had finally disembarked at Brindisi, Holmes was positively cheery and he rubbed his hands together with enthusiasm once we had discovered that a train bound for Rome would be departing within the hour. For once the schedule proved to be an accurate one, and fifteen hours later our train pulled into the terminus of Rome

We had not the time to forewarn Gialli of our imminent arrival and so we hoped that there would be transportation available at the station, despite the lateness of our arrival. In this we were fortunate also, and the final leg of our journey proved to be a most handsome landau pulled by four.

We had maintained our rooms at the hotel upon the Via Nazionale, which was just as well, for when we did finally arrive at the reception it was in the dead of night. We were certainly glad of our beds that night and when we did finally awake, late on the following morning, we were met by the heartening news that Inspector Gialli would be joining us for a late breakfast.

The poor chap was almost unrecognizable from the immaculately dapper gentleman that we had once known. The wounds upon his face, although clearly well on their way to being healed, were so deep that I was convinced that he would be permanently scarred by them. The sparkle that had once illuminated his eyes was now nothing more than a dark vision of pain and melancholy.

When he shuffled slowly into the dining room, his wave was half-hearted and his smile was nothing more than a pale imitation of his former warm and welcoming countenance. He joined us at our table but in common with my friend he did not partake of the inviting platter of crusty rolls, fruit and cheese, and instead made a small cup of coffee suffice.

Gialli and Holmes waited patiently while I ate my fill, and once the plates had been removed Holmes indicated a small, discreet table in the lounge from where he was certain that we would not be overheard.

'Signori, do not be so dismayed at the sight of my injuries, for they are well on their way to a full recovery and remember that danger is part and parcel of our profession. As you can see I do not intend to leave myself so vulnerable in the future.' After making his ineffective attempt at allaying our fears for his well-being, Gialli pointed towards the far corner of the room. Sure enough, there sat two of Gialli's junior colleagues who seemed to be maintaining a stoic vigil over their commander.

'Now please, Mr Holmes, you must outline to me every detail of your adventures since we last met,' Gialli implored with an eager anticipation.

Under the circumstances, it would have been churlish for us not to have granted Gialli his simple request. As you might imagine this took some little time, for there was much to relate, and Holmes left the majority of this burden to me, while he smoked his pipe in silence with his eyes tightly closed.

'You must excuse me, Inspector; I trust that you will not mistake my intense concentration for boredom and slumber. It is quite often beneficial for me to hear previous events précised for me in such a fashion, as it is not inconceivable, although highly unlikely, that I might have missed a vital clue in the heat of a moment,' Holmes explained with his customary humility!

At this point he decided to take up the tale himself, as we had reached a moment that he considered to be of greater significance, namely our discussions with the venerable Shenouda. Gialli leant forward and hung on to every one of Holmes's remarkable and illuminating words. Gradually, as Holmes began to repeat some of Shenouda's quotations from the Gospel, Gialli seemed to be gaining an insight into the significance of its theft.

'Mr Holmes, thank you for recounting what has undoubtedly been a most remarkable adventure. I must admit, however, that it was my own short-sightedness that made such a long journey so necessary. Had I displayed greater awareness, you would undoubtedly have received that translation right here in Rome.'

'Inspector Gialli, you are being far too hard on yourself!' Holmes proclaimed. 'When you set out for our hotel on that fateful morning, you had no reason to suppose that your mission might have warranted so vicious an attack. There was no obvious reason for you to imagine that anyone outside of the papal enclave would have had an understanding of the scroll's importance and its value.

'You may console yourself with the fact that your injuries precipitated our journey to Egypt, where we have gained considerably more than simply an understanding of the Gospel of Mary. Perhaps you would now reciprocate and report to us any progress that you might have made with your investigation into the death of Cardinal Tosca.'

Gialli bowed in appreciation of Holmes's generous response, before shaking his head dejectedly.

'Mr Holmes, I am afraid that there is precious little to report that you do not already know. Regarding the assault that I suffered, I am only able to confirm the information that you received from my colleague on the day of my attack. My assailants seemed to be quite clear about the object of their foray, for they made no effort to extract my wallet, nor did they conduct a search of my pockets to see if I was conveying anything else of value.

'I could not say how they came by their knowledge, but I am in little doubt that they knew exactly what I was carrying and the motive behind my mission. As to their identity, well, I can only say with any certainty that they hail from your own country of origin. Their costumes were undoubtedly of

English design and their accents were unmistakable,' Gialli concluded.

'I take it, therefore, that you have made no further progress with your investigation into the death of Cardinal Tosca?' Holmes asked with the nonchalance of someone who already knew the answer to his question.

Gialli shook his head dejectedly.

'What about the murder weapon, Inspector? Surely an object of such deadly proportions cannot be too hard for you to locate?' Holmes persisted.

'I am afraid that it could be anywhere by now, Mr Holmes,' Gialli replied forlornly.

'Not so, Inspector! As a matter of fact, I will go so far as to say that the weapon has never even left the building!' Holmes declared dramatically.

'Oh, come along, Holmes, you cannot possibly be implying that the murderer would attempt to conceal such a weapon within the walls of an institution such as the Vatican!' I exclaimed in disbelief.

'I am not just implying it, Watson, I would state categorically that it would be far easier to hide the sword within the Vatican than it would be to remove it and remain unnoticed. You will, no doubt, remember that the door to Cardinal Tosca's office was found locked and that the key had been removed.' This last statement of Holmes seemed to be directed solely towards Gialli, who visibly blushed as he recollected his earlier oversight.

'Yes, but Mr Holmes, why would the murderer go to the bother of forcing the window with his blade, when he could have gained an easier access simply by using the key?' Gialli asked.

'A closer examination of the damage to the frame would have revealed to you, as it did to me, Inspector, that the angle of the blade could only have been made from the inside!'

'From the inside?' the befuddled policeman repeated. Then after a moment of thought an air of realization seemed to come upon him.

'Well, this certainly changes our perspective of the case and drastically narrows the range of our search.' Holmes smiled benignly at Gialli, for he knew long ago that which had only just dawned upon both Gialli and me.

'Inspector, had you ever heard mention of or a reference to an entity known as the unholy trinity?' Holmes asked, rather surprisingly.

'Why yes, Mr Holmes, one of my assailants screamed that phrase out to me by way of a warning, but I thought very little about it at the time, due to my circumstances,' Gialli conceded.

'That is quite understandable, I would say.'

Holmes grunted impatiently at what he no doubt saw as my unnecessary, albeit sympathetic, interruption.

'Watson, you realize, of course, that the inspector's warning confirms our theory that Professor Sydney is one of the three. The murderer of Cardinal Tosca is another, but the third is yet a mystery to me.' Holmes's voice tailed away wistfully as his ceaseless mind continued to grapple with the problem.

'But, Holmes, you have not yet revealed the name of Cardinal Tosca's murderer!' I exclaimed in a state of some exasperation.

Whether it was intentional or not, Holmes's expression of surprise, at our inability to reach the same conclusion as he had done, was infuriating in the extreme.

'Oh, but is it not yet obvious to you?' he asked us in a similar vein, while, with an obvious air of disdain, he watched us shake our heads in unison.

Our silence was answer enough for Holmes.

'Very well then, our murderer is someone who not only has the ability to translate from ancient Aramaic but he is also someone with the understanding to realize that some of the passages of the Gospel of Mary Magdalene were of greater significance than the remainder. I can assure you that the missing passages were those that Shenouda brought so colourfully to our attention.

'He is also someone who can come and go, within the corridors of the Vatican, without drawing attention to himself and he would not look out of place when gaining access to Cardinal Tosca's office with a key and departing in the same way. It would not have been difficult for him to conceal the blade beneath his long and flowing robes, safe in the knowledge that no one would ever deign to instigate a search of his inner sanctum.'

Gialli's head dropped to his chest as he realized the enormity of the task that now lay ahead of him.

'Holmes, you do realize what you are asking us to believe?' I asked. Although the facts seemed to point in only one direction, it was still hard for me to acknowledge the stark and literal truth.

Holmes slowly lit a cigarette and he smiled at the two of us with an air of relief and satisfaction.

'You see, Cardinal Pietro was always more of a politician than Tosca ever wanted to be. While Tosca saw the scrolls merely as an object of interest and learning, Pietro was able to recognize the threat that their publication would undoubtedly pose to the entire edifice of the Roman Catholic Church.

'Furthermore, and more damningly, Pietro saw them as a weapon to use against Tosca in their struggle to succeed the current Pope. It has long been recognized, within the Vatican's dark corridors of power, that Cardinal Tosca was the natural successor to Pope Leo VIII.

'However, Pietro also knew that if he could prove that Tosca was viewing the Gospel as a viable alternative to the accepted New Testament, then he would have had no great difficulty in discrediting him and therefore he would have been able to usurp Tosca's position in the papal hierarchy.

'Obviously he used a curved blade as a means of implicating the Orthodox Copts, while at the same time ingratiating himself with the Catholic Coptic Patriarch, Makarios.'

Each startling phrase of Holmes's had followed in rapid succession of each other, and by the time that he had concluded, he had rendered himself quite breathless and agitated. His first cigarette had burnt its way through, without having been pulled upon once, and Holmes soon lit another while he watched our reaction to his revelations.

'Surely it would have been sufficient if Pietro had simply discredited Tosca, without him having to resort to murder?' I asked.

I noticed that Gialli had remained silent throughout this entire exchange, as he realized that the task of denouncing Cardinal Pietro would doubtless fall to him.

'I am sure that murder would not have been his first or preferred option, but he brought the blade along in case Tosca refused to hand over the more sensitive passages of the Gospel,' Holmes explained.

'Perhaps Cardinal Tosca even threatened to present his findings to like-minded colleagues or even to the Pope himself?' Gialli suggested.

'Undoubtedly that threat would have precipitated Pietro's act of violence. His perception of the situation would have left him with no other solution than the death of Cardinal Tosca.' I paused as an abhorrent notion suddenly occurred to me. 'Holmes, I trust that you are not suggesting that His Holiness is, in some way, involved in, or might even be the instigator, of Pietro's murderous schemes?'

'I do not suppose for an instant that His Holiness is the third member of the unholy trinity, if that is at the root of your question, Watson. However, his suggestion to me that I should not believe in the existence of more than the four recognized Gospels does seem to imply that he had some knowledge of the nature of Tosca's studies and had good reason to wish that his work cease immediately.

'Although my meeting with the man was only brief, I learned enough about him for me to be able to confirm that he would never sanction an act as impious as that of murder. However, I am equally certain that if the Gospel of Mary Magdalene were to remain hidden for all of time, he would not have any regrets.'

Gialli and I emitted long, low whistles of disbelief as Holmes concluded his summary of the events within the Vatican. Furthermore, we both assumed that this also brought to an end his investigation into the death of Cardinal Tosca. Therefore, my dismay at his next announcement can be well understood.

'Now, Watson, we must arrange our return to London with all speed, for I am sure that you realize that our work has barely begun!'

I looked across at Gialli for some kind of inspiration, but he merely shrugged his slight shoulders and appeared to have been as confused as I was. Besides, he was now faced with the seemingly insoluble problem of how to expose Cardinal Pietro without causing his own destruction.

We three sat in a contemplative silence, for what seemed to be an eternity, before Inspector Gialli finally spoke.

'Once again, Mr Holmes, I find myself in your debt, although, on this occasion, you have risked far more than your reputation!'

Holmes shook his head solemnly.

'No, Inspector, I have merely solved the mystery of the death of Cardinal Tosca. Sadly, the task of exposing Cardinal Pietro falls to you. My part in this affair cannot be made generally known if I am to continue with my work in London with impunity.'

Then, as if in response to my earlier expression of surprise, Holmes added, 'Oh yes, Watson, there is still the small matter of the unholy trinity and its mysterious third member to be resolved. You will be glad to hear that the wires, which I have been sending at regular intervals to my brother Mycroft, will have already set the wheels in motion by the time that we finally arrive back in London.'

'Are you certain that you do not wish your name to appear at all?' Gialli asked with a mixture of embarrassment and perplexity.'

'No, Inspector, not at all. You may inform your superiors and His Holiness that the Englishman was somewhat out of his depth, on this occasion. I would also add Father Bettega to your bag, without any further delay!'

'Father Bettega?' Gialli queried.

'Oh, without a doubt. His ambition is only matched by that of his master and it would have been far easier for him to obtain a key to Cardinal Tosca's office door, as he had Tosca's absolute although undeserved trust.'

As Gialli rose to go about his unenviable task, I could not contain a laugh of amazement for another instant.

'Holmes, we have travelled many hundreds of miles and seen and experienced enough to last a lifetime, yet you had already solved the mystery of Cardinal Tosca's death after a brief examination of his office and a few words with Cardinal Pietro!' I exclaimed.

'Nevertheless, our journey to Egypt was absolutely essential,' Holmes responded. 'After all, without our subsequent understanding of the contents of the missing Gospel, the evidence against Cardinal Pietro would have remained as nothing more than circumstantial. The knowledge that we have accrued in Egypt has not only provided us with a motive for Tosca's murder, but has led us upon the trail of the mysterious unholy trinity.

'Without appearing to denigrate the importance of the events in Rome, I am convinced that our investigation into the trinity will prove to be of a far greater moment!' Holmes declared as he rose to bid our Roman friend a fond farewell.

'One final piece of advice before you take your leave, Inspector. When you confront both the cardinal and his accomplice, ensure that you do so alone!' Holmes would not be drawn any further as to the true meaning of this warning, but I was convinced that he still held reservations as to the loyalty of De Rossi and Gialli left the room in a greater state of perplexity as a result.

I followed him shortly afterwards as Holmes immediately despatched me to instigate our travel arrangements for the journey back to London. It would be several weeks before we received further news from Rome and when we did finally read Gialli's final report, we were safely ensconced in our rooms in Baker Street once more.

It was succinct and to the point, although Gialli had allowed himself the luxury of over-elaborating upon his gratitude to Holmes yet again. Gialli had trodden upon his diplomatic eggshells with both guile and a strong sense of justice that appealed to Holmes but also enhanced his own position and reputation.

The likelihood of a public arrest and trial had always been a remote one. Any revelations as to the contents of the missing documents were going to be damaging to the entire Roman Catholic institution and the Pope would not see a senior cardinal of his humbled publicly. Nevertheless, Gialli was not prepared to see this heinous crime go unpunished and both Pietro and Bettega were required to give up their positions within the Vatican with immediate effect.

Several weeks after their departure, news was received, from the depths of Central Africa, of a missionary and his assistant who had both arrived from Italy with a pledge to devote the remainder of their lives to the spreading of the Gospel amongst the heathens of the Dark Continent, never to return.

CHAPTER THIRTEEN

OUR JOURNEY HOME

HOLMES WAS AS anxious to complete the journey home with the same urgency as he had when we were planning our outward expedition.

With this in mind, I had tried to mirror the exact route that we had taken to Rome, and after much enquiry, within a few hours we found ourselves upon a train to Turin. Although the promptness of our departure had been pleasing to Holmes, it proved to be no consolation for the fact that this particular train seemed to be scheduled to stop at every inconsequential, rural station that we approached.

As a result, I saw very little of Holmes throughout that entire laborious journey. He spent most of his time walking ceaselessly, up and down the corridors, and he drew the attention of most of our fellow passengers as they viewed his unusual behaviour with quizzical eyes.

It goes without saying that he refused food whenever the notion was suggested to him and his consumption of tobacco was nothing less than titanic. I was at a loss as to how I could refocus his attention away from our protracted journey time, when a method suddenly presented itself to me, but in a manner that was most disturbing.

After I had spent several hours observing Holmes's erratic behaviour, I slowly became aware that two of our fellow passengers were affording him more than just a casual glance of surprise. Indeed, they were studying him with what I can only describe as a most disconcerting amount of attention that struck me as being almost sinister.

Then a clue as to their probable identities suddenly occurred to me. They were both dressed impeccably in dark brown, English-cut suits, which had been the exact attire of Inspector Gialli's two assailants! Furthermore, when I had overheard them ordering coffee from the buffet car a while earlier, their accents unmistakably confirmed that they both hailed from London, or its suburbs.

As far as I was concerned the appearance of these two most singularly dressed gentlemen, aboard our train, was beyond mere coincidence and I set off at once to inform Holmes of my discovery. I became somewhat agitated when there was no sign of him at either of his two favourite haunts, namely his sleeping berth and the observation car. There was no trace of the stench of his tobacco at either of these locations and once I had realized that it had been some time since I had seen the two men in brown, I became terribly concerned for Holmes's safety.

I intensified my search for him but decided that it would be indiscreet of me were I to involve either of the guards in my hunt. I traversed the length of the corridors several times before I became convinced that the men in brown had made away with Holmes over the side of the train!

I had made up my mind to inform the guards of my fears and I was on the point of summoning them to my side when I heard a most familiar voice coming from behind a closed compartment door. I pulled out my revolver and barged the door open with my good shoulder.

'It is certainly good of you to join us, Watson, although I do wish that you had chosen to make a somewhat less dramatic and noisy entrance!' Holmes greeted me with an air of surprising joviality.

I froze in disbelief as I observed the scenario in front of me from the doorway to the small room. The two men in brown were seated, somewhat uncomfortably, on the seats to my right while Holmes faced them with a small pocket pistol, which he occasionally carried for such a contingency, trained upon the head of the man sitting closest to him.

Once I could see that Holmes had this situation fully in hand, I decided to return my revolver to its pocket and wait for Holmes's explanation of this latest development.

'I must confess, Watson, that from the moment that they came aboard the train, I was aware of the potential danger that their presence posed—'

I had taken my eyes off Holmes's captives just for the briefest moment, while I took my seat next to him. In that instant one of the men in brown made a desperate lunge towards Holmes and the ruffian managed to knock the pistol from Holmes's hand, while he was still in mid-sentence.

Perhaps my entrance into the berth had distracted Holmes from the matter in hand, for I could think of no other reason for Holmes's uncharacteristic lapse in concentration. Be that as it may, the roles had now been reversed and Holmes now had his own pistol trained upon him! I decided to divert some attention away from Holmes and moved back towards the door before the man with the gun was able to back away from us.

'Kindly remove your revolver, Doctor Watson, and slide it towards me, before I blow a hole clean through your friend's head!'

Both men were rather tall and burly, so it was hard to reconcile that so thin and reedy a voice could emanate from such a source. Nevertheless it was this aspect of his command that made it sound all the more chilling. It left me in little doubt that he had every intention of carrying out his threat should I refuse to do his bidding.

Consequently, I was on the point of placing my hand in my pocket once more when Holmes suddenly barked out a counter command.

'No, Watson, they cannot possibly shoot us both with such a weapon, and you will surely have your gun ready before it can be reloaded.'

'Holmes, I will not let them shoot you!' I shouted, while discreetly easing my revolver from its pocket.

'Give up your revolver and all will surely be lost. I beseech you, bring it to bear upon these rogues, so that one of us, at least, can carry on our work in London.'

I could feel a bead of perspiration building up on my fore-head, for the prospect of losing Holmes loomed larger than the idea of defying him once again. Nevertheless there was a tone in his voice that I had heard many times before and it induced in me a great act of trust. I did remove my revolver, but instead of handing it over I brought it to bear upon the man who was now threatening Holmes.

'You are a fool, Doctor Watson, if you think that my threat was an empty one.' A chill went through me as the man spat out these alarming words and my heart shuddered as he pulled the trigger....

Holmes still sat there, placidly and calmly, and he flashed a brief and knowing smile as he reached up to reclaim his weapon. The man was struck with horror as the tiny trigger struck against a silent and empty chamber and he allowed the gun to fall from his hand and into Holmes's.

I moved closer towards them all and made sure the two men understood my intention to use my revolver if either of them made a move. Despite the intensity of my actions, the man with the reedy voice was not to be so easily convinced.

'You have no intention of shooting us, Doctor Watson, I am certain of it,' he hissed while exposing a hideous line of tiny green teeth that appeared to have been filed down to a point.

'You forget that I have fought in the Afghan campaign, during the course of which I have fired upon far more worthy human beings than yourselves! Now back into your seats at once!' I ordered while pulling back the trigger with my thumb.

Holmes clapped his hands together resonantly in triumph.

'Bravo, Watson, bravo! Once again you have risen to the occasion and saved the day, not to mention my life.'

'Surely you achieved that yourself, by ensuring that your pistol remained empty of bullets,' I replied, feeling somewhat embarrassed by Holmes's heartfelt applause. 'How else could you have remained so calm while peering down the barrel of a gun and then encourage me to retain possession of my own?'

Holmes cleared his throat and responded to my question somewhat sheepishly.

'I am ashamed to admit, Watson, that what you perceive as an act of hindsight was nothing more than an impulsive oversight on my part!'

The two strangers exchanged glances that indicated that they were as exasperated as I felt upon hearing Holmes's inconceivable admission.

'I cannot believe that once again you have jeopardized your own life in so cavalier a fashion!' I was certain that my remonstrations had been expressed in vain, although this time, at least, Holmes did appear somewhat abashed.

By now the two men in brown had begun to shift around uncomfortably on their seats, doubtlessly trying to fathom out their eventual fates. In truth, I was also unsure of Holmes's intentions and we all turned towards him to discover how this situation was going to be resolved.

'Watson, you shall be relieved to discover that I was aware of the presence of these dubious gentlemen, long before your own moment of realization. Consequently, at our last port of call and while the engine was taking water on board, I had the time and opportunity to despatch two most timely wires.

'Consequently, when we do finally arrive in Paris, our next and final station, my old friend Berlajous, together with his finest officers, will be awaiting our arrival at the platform armed with two sets of cufflinks. Once these two have been safely secured and in the hands of an escort, they will be put aboard the very next train to Turin where they will be well met by a most anxious Inspector Gialli, who is, of course, the recipient of my second wire! As to the fate that he has in mind for them, one can only speculate upon.' Holmes concluded by flashing a most malicious smile in the direction of our hapless captives.

'You seem to have arranged everything most admirably, Holmes, and I congratulate you. However, we have yet to learn how they came by their knowledge and the nature of Gialli's package, much less the identity of their influential employer,' I reminded him.

'Well, Watson, the outcome to this conundrum seems to rest very much with our prisoners,' Holmes replied enigmatically.

'I do not understand how the fates of two such scoundrels should rest in their own hands. The very idea is nothing sort of scandalous!' I exclaimed.

'Calm yourself, old friend, for you misunderstand me. It is for them to decide as to whom they would regard as their preferred interrogators. After all, Gialli was the victim of a most callous and violent attack and therefore he might have in mind his own methods of extracting evidence.'

I now fully understood Holmes's ploy, for he was

undoubtedly trying to unnerve the two rogues with his veiled threats of violence at the hands of our Italian colleague. In this, however, he was only partially successful. The larger of the two, who was still yet to speak, immediately rose to Holmes's bait. He jumped up excitedly and before his colleague could prevent him, began to gabble nervously.

'That damnable little Italian will have us, I tell you, and if he does not, well, then your Bavarian Brotherhood certainly will!'

The man with the reedy voice suddenly reached across and grabbed his colleague by the throat.

'You fool! If they do not have you then I certainly will! You have already said far too much and placed us both in jeopardy. Can you not see that this fellow is playing a game that he cannot win? That inspector is powerless against the forces that protect us. Let them send us back to Italy, for all the good that will do them, but I warn you, if you value your life do not utter another solitary word!'

That awful fellow uttered his caution with such maliciousness and spite that I felt the hairs rise upon the back of my neck. None of us were left in any doubt that he meant every word and his associate sat down again without a moment's hesitation. 'These two are not members of the official force and I will be damned if we should assist them in any way.' The man with the pointed teeth issued this final warning to the other.

As a consequence, in spite of all of our efforts and threatening behaviour, neither of our captives could be persuaded to speak again prior to our arrival in Paris. For the remainder of the journey Holmes and I exchanged duties with my revolver and ensured that our prisoners were not left alone for an instant.

As was his wont, Holmes maintained the majority of this vigil, so that I might make use of the dining car and take a little rest. Thankfully there were no further stops before our arrival in Paris.

By the time that we finally completed our journey, all of Holmes's plans had been put into place and Berlajous and his men immediately came aboard to take possession of our charges. I, for one, was not sorry to see the back of them.

'Mr Holmes, you are a fool if you perceive this as a success. You have embarked upon a road that can only lead to your inevitable destruction!' The odious creature with the deformed teeth spat out this final warning as his wrists were being cuffed together behind his back.

Neither of them struggled as they were being led from the train and they both displayed an unruffled confidence that I found to be somewhat disconcerting. Before he made his way to the train for Turin, Berlajous confirmed that Gialli and his men would be prepared to receive the prisoners upon their arrival in Italy and, confident that we had achieved all that we could, Holmes and I set about making our arrangements for the boat train back to London.

'I am appalled at their behaviour,' I complained. 'After all, anyone would suppose that they were the victors and not the victims!'

Our train would not be ready for boarding for an hour or so, so Holmes and I used this time in despatching our final wire back to London and taking a cup of coffee.

'I am sure that their confidence will prove to be misguided and that Gialli will know precisely how to deal with them,' Holmes assured me.

'Well, I wish I could share your opinion. After all, they would not be drawn towards answering even one of our questions and we are no better off than we were before.'

Holmes smiled benignly at me as he slowly lit a cigarette.

'Really, Watson?' Holmes encouraged me to answer my own query.

'Of course, the Bavarian Brotherhood!' I exclaimed in sudden realization. 'But what does that mean and who are the Brotherhood?'

'I assure you, Watson, that I do not have the foggiest notion!' Holmes laughed. 'However, I have every intention of finding out as soon as we arrive back in London.'

'I am much relieved, although a little surprised that you did not propose that we are to travel next to Bavaria,' I said, with a strong sense of irony in my voice.

'No, Watson, I am now convinced that the remainder of this affair will finally be resolved in London.' Holmes smiled and for once I think that he understood the humour behind my previous statement.

'It is indeed most ironic, is it not, that after all that we have endured and survived in those exotic lands, the final solution lies within a few miles of Baker Street?' Holmes suggested.

I could not think of a single, feasible reply to Holmes's most singular statement and a short while later we were boarding the boat train: the final leg of a most extraordinary journey. Furthermore, it was also the smoothest and most expeditious stage that we had enjoyed and an unseasonably calm Channel assured us of a most benign and pleasant crossing.

It felt strange to me when we finally arrived at Charing Cross Station, because nothing really seemed to have changed since our departure, save for Holmes and I. It was almost as if our experiences of the last few weeks had not actually taken place and that we had merely lived through a bizarre and surreal dream. It was only the steely intent in the eyes of my friend, which I noticed as we slowly alighted from the train, that reminded me of the task that still lay ahead of us.

It was a pleasant surprise to discover that our old comrade, Dave 'Gunner' King, and his cab were waiting for us outside, for I was not even aware that he knew of our time of arrival. This feeling was compounded further by Holmes's reaction to

King's explanation for his being there.

'Don't worry, Doctor Watson, I've not been waiting here all the time that you have been away,' he laughed. 'Mr Holmes's brother has made all of the arrangements. To Baker Street, Mr Holmes?'

'With all speed, Gunner King!' Holmes commanded as King helped us load up our luggage.

I was already in the cab when, to my great surprise, Holmes suddenly ignored the welcoming vehicle and ran towards a four-foot-high retaining wall that surrounded the station. With a single athletic leap, he landed sure-footedly upon the narrow ledge at its top. Then with his back straightened and his neck erect, he gazed skyward longingly and he smiled as though enwrapped by an awesome yet invisible force.

He summoned me to join him and I stared towards Holmes from the base of the wall.

'Can you not sense and feel it, Watson?' he asked quietly, with his stoic attitude unchanged.

I slowly shook my head in disappointed surprise and glanced back towards King, who was calming his impatient and agitated horse with unusually gentle strokes of his hand, up and down the length of the animal's neck.

'I have been fortunate enough to have visited many cities around the world, both in your company, Watson, and on my own. However, I have yet to experience the rich tapestry of culture and the vibrant flux of life that seems to permeate each one of London's colourful thoroughfares and its darkest alleys.

'During the course of the many and diverse adventures that you and I have experienced together, we have had to both burrow through to this city's vilest underbelly and also risen to its dizziest and most dazzling summits. However, on this occasion I fear that we may have to ascend to Olympus herself before we are done!' It was only now that Holmes lowered his gaze towards me and his eyes seemed to be penetrating into my innermost being, as if trying to gauge whether I was up to this, our ultimate challenge.

He was obviously satisfied that I was, for as he leapt down from the wall he clouted the centre of my back with his palm and emitted a cheer of triumph.

'The die then is cast, Watson. To 221b Baker Street if you please, King!'

CHAPTER FOURTEEN

INSPECTOR LESTRADE

I MUST ADMIT that the welcome we received from Mrs Hudson upon our return to Baker Street was not exactly the warmest that we might have expected, considering the circumstances of our protracted absence.

She scowled down at us both from the doorstep while we struggled with our luggage, as a mother might react towards her badly behaved children. However, she quickly relented and the relief that she displayed at our safe return soon became apparent, despite her scolding words.

'What a lot of tomfoolery, I would say, asking me to remain inside my own house with you two gallivanting all over the place! Much chance I had for some peace and quiet, with all those policemen calling round at every hour of the day and night! It is nothing more than stuff and nonsense; I am in greater danger when you are both in residence!' She had her arms crossed belligerently in front of her, but she failed to conceal a warm affectionate smile for very long.

'We are equally glad to see you, Mrs Hudson, especially if there is a chance of a bite or two. I am absolutely ravenous!' Although I was only teasing her, my statement was certainly not too wide of the mark.

We were both grateful to note that the door to our rooms had been fully restored, although we still remained short of one chair. Mrs Hudson hoped that one of a huge pile of letters that awaited Holmes's attention would contain the anticipated cheque from the Netherlands so that she might be compensated for the expensive repairs.

She ushered us through the door, rather unceremoniously, and before too long a table full of cold meats and bread was spread before us. As she was at the point of leaving the room, Mrs Hudson begged our indulgence for a moment or two longer.

'I should warn you, gentlemen, that you might very well be receiving a call from that awful Inspector Lestrade before too long. He has enquired about your anticipated return every day for a week or more and I daresay he has a case or two that might require your attention. In fact, he has been around so often that I thought he was going to ask me to solve the case for him!'

'It would be no surprise to me if you were to prove more successful than he!' Holmes laughed. 'Now, run along, Mrs Hudson, and thank you for the warning.' Our landlady was still laughing even as Holmes was marshalling her out of the room.

'Inspector Lestrade?' I murmured through a mouthful of ham. 'The last time you returned after a long absence he presented you with a case that led to the arrest of Colonel Sebastian Moran.' I was, of course, referring to the most singular assassination of the Honourable Ronald Adair that featured in a story I entitled 'The Empty House'.

'Anything that turns out to be even half as stimulating might be worthy of your attention,' I suggested.

'Well, well, well, so Scotland Yard's finest still cannot function without the aid of their old consulting detective!'

Holmes declared gleefully.

I should make mention, at this point, of the transformation that had taken place in the relationship between Holmes and Lestrade, ever since the case of the 'Six Napoleons'. Up to that moment in their history, there had always been an element of mistrust between the two and a sense that each of them was playing a game of brinkmanship with the other.

While this was probably true, it can also be said that this was a most one-sided game indeed, as Holmes emerged as the victor on every occasion. However, Lestrade had been so impressed with the 'workmanlike' nature of Holmes's investigation into the broken busts that all feelings of resentment had been dispelled from that point onwards and they now harboured a concealed respect for the other.

Consequently, Holmes and I were now awaiting Lestrade's visit with an invigorating anticipation that we had not experienced previously. As it transpired, this was destined to be for another time, and we continued with our supper without further interruption.

Once our simple meal had been concluded and we had changed into more comfortable garments, Holmes and I retired to our customary chairs by the fire with a glass of port and our pipes in hand.

There was something strangely comforting in the sight of Holmes draped within his familiar purple dressing gown and holding his elegant cherry wood. We both became transfixed by the glow of the crackling embers within the fireplace and for a few moments at least, all thoughts of stolen parchments and Bavarian Brotherhoods were dispelled.

It was I who eventually broke the silence and shattered that rare moment of tranquillity.

'How do you propose that we proceed in the morning?'

Holmes withdrew his pipe and turned to me with a familiar look of frustration in his eyes.

'I am afraid that, at the moment, there is no other course of action open to us but to wait. My brother has promised to unearth as much information as he can in regard to the background and the whereabouts of Professor Ronald Sydney. Only once he has done so will we be able to act,' Holmes said dejectedly.

'Surely in the meantime we can attempt to discover the nature of this brotherhood that the man in the brown suit so colourfully referred to?' I suggested. 'After all, he did seem to attach much credence to its influence.'

'Perhaps a little too much for my liking. However, it is hard to forge a direct link between Sydney and an obscure Germanic clan without their making a move towards us first. Only then will we be able to understand their intentions and their motives.'

'Surely by then it might be too late!' I protested. Holmes studied me for a moment before responding.

'Well, I suppose that a wire to a colleague or two in that part of the world may not be out of order,' Holmes conceded with surprising reluctance.

'Well, I for one would be glad to know who or what we might be dealing with,' I said as I slowly rose from my chair. 'Will you be retiring shortly?' I asked through a long yawn, although I was reasonably certain that the exact opposite would prove to be the case.

'You go ahead, old fellow. I favour the idea of another pipe or two, myself,' came his inevitable reply and he turned back towards the fire, which seemed to contain some form of inspiration for him.

'Good night, Holmes,' I called out softly on my way up to my room, with no expectation of a response.

When I eventually came down on the following morning, I was most surprised to note that Holmes had actually vacated his chair at some point during the night and that he had decided to take to his bed. One glance at his overflowing ashtray showed me that this had been a most belated decision and therefore I did not anticipate seeing him again until well into the afternoon.

I took a quiet breakfast on my own and then decided to take an extended walk while I set about collecting our morning newspapers. As I strolled along the bustling thoroughfare that was the Marylebone Road, I began to understand the meaning behind Holmes's strange speech from atop the wall at Charing Cross Station of the night before.

There was undoubtedly a diversity of race and creed, of the wealthy and the impoverished, of the slovenly and the well-dressed industrious, that one would seldom experience in other major cities around the globe. I found that it was most invigorating to be a part of such a heaving flux of humanity and I could not help but wonder at the stories behind each of the external persona that I passed along my route.

I felt excited at the thought of finding one of their stories within my notebook one day and wished that I could share Holmes's amazing insight into such matters. Surely by now he would have been able to identify the vocations of dozens of these passers-by, information that would remain a mystery to everyone apart from he.

By the time I had returned to our front door, I was certain that I was now ready for whatever eventuality fate, or indeed the Bavarian Brotherhood, might happen to throw in our direction. I completed the ascent of the seventeen steps that led to our rooms in six bounds and I was thrilled at the prospect of Holmes sharing my enthusiasm.

Sadly, I was to remain disappointed, for a short while longer at least. For instead of finding my old friend sitting in his chair by the fire, there was our former adversary, Inspector Lestrade of Scotland Yard, squirming impatiently in his place.

He shot out of his seat in a heartbeat at the sight of me entering the room.

'Oh, Doctor Watson, so it is true! You and Mr Holmes have finally returned from … wherever it is that you went to!'

Lestrade's excitement at seeing me soon turned into confusion as he suddenly realized that he had not a single clue as to where we had travelled to during our protracted absence. Under our present set of circumstances, I had absolutely no intention of enlightening him and merely greeted him with a handshake and a smile.

'Yes, Inspector, it is true, although I believe that Mr Holmes is still in the process of taking some well-earned rest,' I said while lowering my voice to a whisper and subtly ushering Lestrade towards our door.

'There is no need for silence and discretion on my behalf, Doctor Watson, for, as you might have observed, I am already wide awake! Good day to you, Inspector Lestrade, you are more than welcome to try my chair,' Holmes greeted him with surprising joviality.

Lestrade and I were equally taken aback by Holmes's sudden entrance into the room, and by his tawdry appearance. He was as far removed from his habitually well-groomed and suited self as one could possibly have imagined.

His unkempt and tousled hair was falling down over his forehead and he was clearly in need of a shave. He was leaning against the doorway to his room dressed only in a badly creased nightshirt. He was clearly chilled, however, and he soon went back inside to fetch his dressing gown, which he draped around his shoulders while he fumbled for a match within the garment's cavernous pockets

I applied one of my own to a cigarette that was hanging apologetically from his dry lips and as he pulled gratefully upon it he sank into the chair that Lestrade had so hastily just vacated. Holmes swept his hair back with his hand and turned towards the bewildered inspector with a smile of expectation.

'Watson, you really have been most remiss by not having sent down for some coffee for our visitor. I see that he might be in some urgent need of refreshment.'

With that Holmes dashed over to the door and called down to Mrs Hudson for a tray of coffee and a jug of hot water. He then sank back into his chair and invited Lestrade to describe his problem, with a crook of his finger and a nod towards the inspector's notebook. Simultaneously, I hurried to fetch a notebook and pencil of my own and then encouraged Lestrade to make use of the spare chair.

'Mr Holmes, it is a pleasure to see that you have made a safe return, but I fail to see how you know that I have a current problem that needs your attention.'

'Inspector, although we have been seeing things on a more eye-to-eye basis in recent times, I am reasonably certain that we have not yet taken to paying social calls upon each other! Besides, Mrs Hudson has kept us up to date on all of your recent comings and goings.'

Lestrade cleared his throat rather awkwardly, bowed in shamed admission and then removed his bowler, which he threw casually down upon the table that sat between us. At that moment our landlady bustled into the room and set down a tray with three cups, before carrying a large steaming jug into Holmes's room.

Holmes leant over and hurriedly poured himself a small coffee, which he drank with an equal haste and lack of ceremony.

'You will, I trust, excuse me while I attend to my toilet, although I will, of course, keep my door open and Watson will take notes.' Holmes pointed to his profuse stubble as an excuse for his bohemian behaviour. 'Now, please, Inspector, describe to me in precise detail each aspect of your problem that you feel might aid me in my enquiries.' This last instruction Holmes bellowed from inside his room. Lestrade's ferret-like features twitched in irritation at what, he no doubt, saw as an affront. I could sympathize with the troubled inspector, as I also found Holmes's outlandish behaviour to be somewhat off-putting. However, we both now opened our notebooks as Lestrade began to read from his in a strident voice that would have been audible to Holmes.

'It is true to say, Mr Holmes, that I do have a problem to present you with, that I trust will appeal to your love of all things that are a little bit off the beaten track. Although you will also be disappointed to learn that the case to which I am referring has already been closed. I am just hoping that, for my own personal satisfaction, you will see this as a question of art for art's sake and solve my little problem as a professional challenge.'

'It will be an honour to assist you in any manner that I am able, Inspector. However, may I sincerely request that you refrain from any further prevarication?' Holmes's response was certainly as loud and as strident as had been Lestrade's opening remarks and I looked forward to the moment when Holmes would conclude his shave and return to the room.

However, that moment was still to be some time in coming and Lestrade was forced to continually raise his voice throughout the early part of his narrative.

'Although I am aware that you have only returned just recently, I am certain that you have no doubt heard of the untimely and tragic death of the misanthrope, Christophe Decaux?'

For an instant Holmes's head poked around the side of his half-opened door and he looked questioningly towards me in search of an answer to Lestrade's challenge. In this, however, I was to sadly disappoint him and my only response was a dejected shaking of my head.

'Really, Mr Holmes, you do surprise me! After all, news of this tragedy has been swamping the national newspapers continually over the last three days.' I could not help but smile at the temporary breakdown in diplomatic relations between Holmes and Lestrade, for there was surely a malicious smile of disdain dancing its way around Lestrade's thin and colourless lips.

'Thank you, Inspector, but you must excuse us. As we have travelled far and have had little time to keep up to date with domestic news, perhaps you would be good enough to enlighten us?' Holmes suggested with a sardonic smile.

'For example, who exactly is this Christophe Decaux and why would you suppose that his demise would be of interest to us, especially as this case has already been officially closed?' I added, much to Holmes's satisfaction.

'Well done, Watson!' The echo that surrounded Holmes's raucous call confirmed to me that his head was still tilted over his wash bowl as he hurried to complete his shave.

'Despite the coroner's verdict, that Decaux's cause of death was accidental, induced by the venom from one of his own snakes, there is one aspect of this case that still perplexes me.'

'Ha! What, pray, would that be, Inspector?' Holmes called out, although he was clearly unable to conceal his amusement at Lestrade's particular turn of phrase. Lestrade decided to ignore Holmes's laughter and pressed ahead with his story.

'Perhaps you might find it to be more beneficial if I were to provide you with a few details that pertain to Decaux and his unusual lifestyle, which might aid you in coming to a conclusion regarding my own most singular little problem?' Lestrade suggested.

'By all means, Inspector.' At that moment Holmes came striding back into the room in a state of some agitation and he made straight towards the top of the mantelpiece whereon he rummaged for his first pipe of the day. Once this was safely alight, Holmes made directly to his chair, which he sat down upon while assuming the classic lotus position. He closed his eyes tightly so that he could maintain the deepest concentration.

Although he was now shaved and dressed, Holmes's shirt collar was still open and there was no sign of his customary tie. Perhaps he was continuing with the style of dress that he assumed while we were in Egypt? As Holmes was now oblivious to his surroundings, it was left to me to encourage Lestrade to begin.

'Christophe Decaux was a man of most singular habits who also maintained many interests, although some might call them obsessions. The fact that he inherited a vast sum of money from an uncle who once held a large stake in a South African diamond mine meant that he possessed both the time and the financial means necessary to indulge these passions.

'For a man of forty-seven years to be so financially secure inevitably led to him becoming quite the eligible bachelor. Despite his misanthropic nature, he eventually succumbed to the advances of one of his pursuants and he was engaged to be married to the beautiful heiress Elizabeth Cowling when this tragedy struck.'

'Hmm, he was certainly moving within some illustrious circles,' I commented while Lestrade rummaged through his notes.

'Indeed he was, Doctor, and he counted amongst his closest friends the heads of some of the leading banking houses of Europe!'

'Yet you describe him as being a man of singularly unsocial habits,' I reminded him.

'From all accounts he was, Doctor. He was very rarely seen in public, save for his frequent visits to his local church, and he spent the majority of his time in cataloguing his collections and paying long and frequent visits to his club, the

Diogenes—' Lestrade was suddenly interrupted by Holmes, who turned towards him with some urgency.

'His local church, you say?' Holmes asked.

'Oh yes, Mr Holmes, he was a devout follower of the Roman Catholic persuasion, probably due to the fact that his family originally crossed the Channel at the time of the Norman conquest. Both of his parents died in a boating accident barely two years ago and he is seen lighting candles, for them both, at least twice a day.'

'What collections would these be?' I asked, surprised that Decaux's visits to his local church interested Holmes more than the man's obsessional interests and, of course, the name of his club!

'He was a dealer in and an avid collector of rare, foreign, antique books, although more pertinently, he was also hell bent on collecting every species of snake that is known to man!'

'Ah, so we finally arrive at the crux of the matter,' Holmes said with just a little impatience.

'Indeed we do, Mr Holmes, although what you will make of it all, heaven only knows.'

'You must explain to me, in the most exact terms that you can, the circumstances surrounding the death of Decaux,' Holmes said quietly, although his eyes were still tightly shut.

Lestrade referred to his notebook most diligently before he spoke next.

'In preparation for his impending marriage, Decaux recently took possession of a large suite of rooms in one of these new, luxury, high-rise buildings, also known as Babylonian buildings, that have been springing up all over central London recently.

'The one in question, Queen Anne's Mansions, in Petty France, is the highest in London and boasts the levels of refinement that would befit a man of Decaux's means and standing. I only mention this, Mr Holmes, so that you will fully appreciate the significance of the sworn evidence of the concierge.' Lestrade was clearly anticipating an impatient reaction from Holmes to his appraisal of Decaux's recently acquired home.

'You attach so much importance to the word of this worthy?' Holmes asked.

'Indeed I do, Mr Holmes, and you will understand why within a moment or two. Along with the rooms, Decaux also took for himself a valet, of a similar age to himself, who had come highly recommended by a fellow member of the Diogenes club. The valet, who went by the name of Roger Ashley, was regarded by all who knew him to be as meticulous as his employer and he was, therefore, the perfect gentleman's gentleman.'

'Well, Lestrade, it seems that the circumstances of our friend, Christophe Decaux, could not possibly have been set any fairer,' Holmes suggested, somewhat cynically.

'Indeed, Mr Holmes, which makes his premature death all the more tragic. On the evening of Thursday last—'
'That would have been the thirteenth, Holmes,' I interjected while referring to my diary.

'On the evening in question, Decaux had decided to make one final visit to his club—'

'I apologize for a further interruption, Inspector, but why was this to be his last night as a member of this illustrious institution?' Holmes asked, while turning towards the inspector for the first time.

'The circumstances of his resignation remain shrouded in mystery, I am afraid. His fiancée knew nothing of the matter whatsoever and as far as Ashley knew Decaux was merely returning for one last time in order to finalize his subscription and bar bills. As you might know, the club adheres to a most stringent code of silence within its walls, so therefore there was nobody amongst its membership who could shed any light upon the matter.'

'I have heard something of the sort,' Holmes confirmed.

'According to Ashley, this visit was to have been a very brief one, as Miss Cowling was due to have joined him for cocktails at nine o'clock and Decaux had arranged for a carriage at eight. Due to the romantic nature of the evening that lay ahead and for the sake of discretion, Ashley had been given the evening off and he left Queen Anne's Mansions at exactly fifteen minutes to the hour.

'The time of his departure was subsequently confirmed by the concierge and we certainly had no reason to doubt his word. The carriage arrived promptly at eight o'clock, but to the surprise of all concerned, there was no sign of Decaux. The man was punctual to a fault, so that by the time the clock had reached a quarter past the hour, his continued absence was beginning to cause great concern. The concierge summoned a page to replace him at the front desk while he went upstairs to investigate.

'He banged upon the door with his fists several times but the door remained closed. All the while he was calling out Decaux's name in the hope that he might receive a response. However, the only sound that he could make out was a soft groan that almost resembled a snore! That decided him and he then attempted to force the door with a series of shoulder barges. Unfortunately for him the quality and thickness of the doors only caused him to damage his shoulder and he summoned the driver for further assistance.

'Eventually the lock gave way and fell to the floor while the door slowly swung open. There, strewn across an ornate Persian rug, was the lifeless form of Christophe Decaux, and after a brief examination, which confirmed his passing, the concierge immediately despatched the page to summon the police.

'I arrived with two constables and a police surgeon within half an hour—'

'By now the time would have been approximately a quarter past the hour of nine, I presume?' Holmes asked, while pointing towards my notebook.

'Exactly on the spot, Mr Holmes. Naturally I examined the room for clues with my usual tenacity and attention to detail and I have to admit that initially I found very little that indicated a cause of death. As we already knew, the door had been securely closed and Decaux's rooms were positioned on the tenth and uppermost floor, so there was absolutely no reason to speculate upon an intruder.

'There were no indications of violence neither within the room nor upon Decaux's person. Therefore, our surgeon began his initial examination on the basis that Decaux had died of natural causes. Obviously this required more time and better facilities than he had available to him there, so he arranged to have the body removed to the mortuary at once.'

'I congratulate you, Lestrade, for your conduct at the scene of the crime was exemplary.' My compliment brought a smile to his face that his pride would not allow him to suppress.

'However, the police surgeon's subsequent examination revealed much more, did it not, Inspector?' Holmes asked and I could sense that his enthusiasm for Lestrade's account was increasing with each passing minute. He abandoned his pipe and faced Lestrade with a cigarette alight and a fire in his eyes.

'Indeed it did, Mr Holmes, although I am not so sure that he would have examined the body in quite the same way had I not discovered the snake during my final examination of the room!'

'I should have been more surprised had there not been one present within the rooms of such an avid collector,' Holmes remarked somewhat cynically.

'Believe me, Mr Holmes, the place was full of every variety that one could imagine. However, each snake was safely locked away within its glass vivarium … save one! We might well have failed to notice it, were it not for my meticulous nature. As I was straightening a chair in the far corner of the room, I noticed an unseemly lump lurking beneath the Persian rug.

'It was fortunate for me that I pulled the corner back with great care, for I slowly revealed, curled up within a tight ball, nothing less than a deadly asp, or aspis, otherwise known as the Egyptian cobra! One bite of this devil is deadly; as a matter of fact death is such a surety that in ancient times its poison was used as a fast and painless form of execution. Neither of us would dare to touch the devil and we had to summon an expert to ensure its safe removal before any further damage could be done.'

'You seem to have become quite the expert upon the subject of snakes, Inspector. Was there no doubt that the bite from this beast was the cause of Decaux's death?' I asked.

'Both the police surgeon and the subsequent coroner's report confirmed the symptoms of death from its bite and the presence of its venom within his blood. Furthermore, the traces of the snake's fang bites are clearly visible upon the back of the dead man's neck.'

'That is rather a high ground for a snake to have taken, is it not?' Holmes asked.

'Under normal circumstances you would be correct, Mr Holmes. However, Mr Decaux's body was found close to a chair that had recently been sat upon and a vacant vivarium, with its door found slightly ajar, that was situated close by to the chair. It is not beyond the capabilities of an asp to have curled its way up the side of a chair and subsequently attack a man's neck.'

'You and the authorities have clearly gone into this matter

most thoroughly and efficiently,' Holmes confirmed, with barely concealed surprise in his voice. 'Was there any consideration given to the notion that he might have committed suicide?'

'Indeed there was, Mr Holmes, but this was dismissed at the coroner's hearing. There was certainly no reason to suppose that somebody in Decaux's situation would consider taking such an awful step. After all, he had only been engaged to be married for a short while, he had recently acquired an expensive and most desirable new home and he was undoubtedly successful in every other aspect of his life,' Lestrade confirmed and I was most impressed by his full possession of the facts.

'Yet he was clearly still grieving over the tragic and premature deaths of his parents and something had surely spurred him into resigning from a most prestigious gentlemen's club,' Holmes suggested.

'Granted, but their deaths did occur over two years ago and the verdict was that after such a long period of time it would hardly be a good enough reason for a man to take so drastic an action. Besides, there was no suicide note found anywhere within his rooms, nor were there any indications from his behaviour that he was close to desperation.

'Due to the most singular nature that is often attributed to the members of the Diogenes club, it is most unlikely that we shall ever discover the true motive behind his desire to resign his membership. However, it was also reasoned that there were no set of circumstances behind such a commonplace action that could possibly induce an act of suicide. The coroner also ruled that if a man were to take his own life in such a manner, there were more convenient parts of the body for him to apply the snake's head to than the back of his neck!'

Throughout the majority of these later exchanges, Lestrade was referring most studiously to the transcript that had been taken at the coroner's hearing. As a consequence we had no good reason to question the validity of his notes and the conclusions that were drawn seemed to have no obvious flaws. Even Holmes appeared to be satisfied by the verdicts that had been reached, yet he still had one final question.

'Inspector Lestrade, throughout your most excellent appraisal of the case, I have not once heard you make mention of the possibility that murder had been the cause of Decaux's death. Was this option not even mentioned once throughout the hearing?'

'Murder, Mr Holmes, murder?' Lestrade could barely conceal his amusement at such a suggestion. 'Oh yes, it was brought up briefly, but it was immediately dismissed out of hand as an inconceivable notion!'

'Why, may I ask, was such a viable possibility dismissed?' Holmes persisted.

'Well, for one thing, who would have been able to commit such a deed? There was nobody else in the room when the tragedy occurred and as we know from the evidence from the concierge, the door to Decaux's rooms was not only locked but almost impossible to break down!

'Furthermore, as I mentioned earlier, Decaux's rooms were located on the tenth floor of the building so, therefore, there was absolutely no possibility of anyone gaining access through a window. No, Mr Holmes, I think that we can safely dismiss murder on this occasion, although I realize that it would certainly appeal to your love of the grotesque,' Lestrade finished rather condescendingly.

'The notion of anyone taking another human life never appeals to me, Inspector. However, we have yet to explore the idea that Roger Ashley, the valet, had an ample opportunity to do away with his employer in such a manner.

'After all, did the concierge not testify to the fact that Ashley was observed leaving the building barely forty-five minutes before Decaux's body was discovered? Even with my limited experience, I would say that would constitute an ample opportunity.'

My friend appeared to be determined to undermine every one of Lestrade's statements and conclusions, although up to now he had met with no success.

'Again, under another set of circumstances you would be correct, Mr Holmes. However, the testimony of two irrefutable experts upon the subject have confirmed that the length of time between the bite from an asp and the inevitable deadly result of such an attack never exceeds a period of fifteen minutes.

'As I am sure you now realize, if Ashley had been the murderer he would have had to remain in Decaux's rooms long after the time indicated by the concierge.' Lestrade concluded his summation with an air of self-satisfaction that even I found to be excruciating and yet, there it was!

'Were these "irrefutable experts" given access to examine the wounds on Decaux's neck?' Holmes persisted.

'They only appeared as expert witnesses. However, the coroner was more than satisfied with the findings of both the police and the mortician at the Chelsea and Westminster Hospital.' By now Holmes's constant questioning was beginning to grate on the inspector's nerves and he fairly spat out his final response.

'You must forgive me, Lestrade, but as you know only too well, I do not accept the existence of coincidence. Perhaps when I hear of a man who dies in a mysterious circumstance and who recently takes into his employ a man who was recommended by a member of a club from which he recently resigns, a mind of my peculiar bent will, by instinct, search for a less than conventional explanation.

'However, on this occasion it would seem that you and the coroner's court have wrapped this matter up very nicely.

In that case I fail to understand why you have come to me today to seek advice that you clearly have very little need of.' Holmes turned away from Lestrade with disdain and walked over to the window.

'As you say, Mr Holmes, the case is closed and the matter is very nicely concluded. Nevertheless, when I returned to Decaux's rooms for one final time, to ensure that we had returned everything to its original order, I was shocked to discover that there had been an oversight after all.'

Holmes abandoned his ennui by the window at once and positively glared down upon the bewildered inspector in anticipation.

'As I mentioned earlier, Decaux was not only an obsessive collector but he was also most meticulous when it came to the cataloguing of these collections.' Inspector Lestrade paused for a moment to catch his breath, for the intensity with which Holmes was staring at him was becoming overbearing.

'Yes, Inspector, please continue. What precisely had been overlooked?'

'During my tidying up I happened to come upon a small ledger in which Decaux had drawn up a dossier for each one of his snakes. Their names, the location at which he had found them and their preferred foods were all listed in precise detail. My interest was only casual and passing, yet even I could not have failed to have noticed a glaring omission from the top of page one.

'There was no entry for an asp!'

Holmes turned away from him again and clapped his hand jubilantly.

'You are certain of this, Lestrade?' he asked him excitedly.

'Oh, absolutely, Mr Holmes! Despite the fact that there was an empty vivarium, and that an asp had been discovered in his room, there was no entry in Decaux's ledger of the very snake that had killed him!'

'I told you before, Lestrade, I do not believe in coincidence. Now tell me, will we still find Christophe Decaux residing within the walls of the mortuary at the Chelsea and Westminster Hospital?'

'Yes indeed, Mr Holmes, the funeral has not been arranged for another two days. Although I must admit that I do not understand your reasons for asking.'

'Despite all of the circumstantial evidence that points towards the verdict of death by misadventure, the fact remains that nobody with the necessary expertise has examined the wounds upon Decaux's neck. I am certain that Doctor Watson here, during his long and arduous tour of duty in Afghanistan, enjoyed that experience on more than one occasion,' Holmes suggested.

'Sadly yes. The Indian cobra is almost identical to its Egyptian counterpart, in every way, and I ministered to its victims on more than one occasion,' I confirmed.

'So, Inspector Lestrade, what say you to an impromptu visit to the Fulham Road? It may prove to be nothing, but we shall surely learn what we may!'

Lestrade and I both nodded our agreement to Holmes's proposal and a moment later we three were all careering down the stairs towards the street below.

Despite the very best efforts of our cab driver, Dave 'Gunner' King, our journey across central London from Baker Street to Fulham Road proved to a drawn-out and most tedious affair. The traffic was nigh on impassable and by the time we had reached Knightsbridge I was contemplating abandoning the cab and proceeding by foot for the remainder of our journey.

I suddenly realized, and with some surprise, that of we three Holmes had remained the most patient and relaxed throughout that travesty of a ride. He was tapping his finger lightly against the wall of the cab in a most rhythmic and harmonious fashion and his serene smile told of a favourite musical phrase that was running through his head.

From that brief observation I could gauge that Holmes had already fashioned an idea of what we were about to discover within the mortuary, which was a lot more than I could say for myself! I could find no valid reason to question the verdict of the coroner's court. Death by misadventure was the only conclusion that seemed to fit all of the facts.

Every alternative explanation that Holmes had put forward was immediately refuted by the evidence from within the notebook of Inspector Lestrade. The fact that Decaux had failed to provide an entry in his ledger for the asp was hardly indicative of foul play! I feared that perhaps Lestrade had been correct on this occasion and that Holmes was indeed searching for something more intriguing than just mere over-sight, which perhaps was not really there.

By the time our cab finally pulled up outside the Chelsea and Westminster Hospital, we were all glad of the opportunity to stretch our legs and take in some fresh air. Then we walked down the length of this imposing building and towards the mortuary that was situated right at the back.

Lestrade had no great difficulty in persuading the mortician to bring out Decaux's corpse for one final examination and before I began to scrutinize the back of his neck, I observed that there had been no indications of fear or anger upon the face of Christophe Decaux, at the moment of his death.

It did not take me long to locate what we had been looking for and upon making my discovery I merely gazed up towards Holmes, while my mouth was gaping wide open in awe.

'How could you have possibly known?' I exclaimed.

'I would not say that I knew exactly, friend Watson, but it was certainly something that I had very much expected you would find. As I informed you both a while earlier, I do not put too much stock in coincidence.'

'I am sorry but I simply do not understand. You have found what exactly, Doctor Watson?' Lestrade's ferret-like face was now horribly contorted by his confusion.

'Why, Inspector, the good doctor has now presented you with your case!' Holmes proclaimed.

'Surely the case is closed, Mr Holmes. What case can you possibly be referring to?'

'I am referring to murder, Inspector Lestrade, in its most cunning and subtle form, admittedly, but murder neverthe-less. Perhaps you would not mind, Doctor.' Holmes ushered Lestrade towards where I was standing that I might indicate to him my discovery.

I pointed down towards two small incisions that were clearly visible in the nape of Decaux's neck.

'You see, Inspector, these marks that purport to be from the fangs of an Egyptian cobra are nothing more than the openings caused by a pair of hypodermic needles, each one attached to a syringe that contained a quantity of the venom of an asp. You can see quite clearly that the spacing that sepa-rates them is too close together for them to have been made by the fangs of a snake. Furthermore, I can find no signs of the slight curvature that is common among all snakes of its type. These marks are far too straight,' I concluded.

'Too straight, too close together, he still died from the venom of an asp,' Lestrade persisted. 'Besides which, there was nobody in Decaux's rooms who might have inserted those syringes.'

'Are you not forgetting about the valet, Roger Ashley?' Holmes asked.

'Ashley was seen leaving the building a full forty-five minutes before Decaux's body was discovered and the venom from an asp takes no longer than fifteen minutes before it becomes effective. I fail to see how Ashley can possibly be implicated in the death of Mr Decaux.'

'By using the syringe, instead of the snake itself, Ashley provided himself with the opportunity of diluting the venom. Naturally, by adjusting the time scale between bite and effect, he was creating for himself the near-perfect alibi,' I suggested.

'Bravo, Watson! You see, Inspector, how the subtlety of this plan indicates that there is mastermind behind the actions of a man who was merely masquerading as a gentleman's valet. He was certainly able to convince the coroner that Decaux died from misadventure.'

'Heavens above, I am sure that he would have succeeded were it not for the intervention of you two gentlemen! Once again I find myself in your debt,' Lestrade commented, although without even a trace of envy or resentment in his voice.

'There will be time enough for congratulations once this affair has been concluded. In the meantime, Inspector, I suggest that you spread your net for Roger Ashley with all speed. Unless I am very much mistaken he will not be remaining within these shores for too much longer.'

'Indeed I will, Mr Holmes, but how can you be so certain of that?'

'Because I think that I can provide you with the names of the very formidable individuals who are behind the actions of Mr Ashley before too long. In the meantime I am certain that they will do everything within their power to keep him out of your clutches,' Holmes concluded thoughtfully.

'I will set my best men upon the task without a moment's delay!'

'Oh, Inspector, perhaps next time you will not accept everything upon its face value. Your work upon this case has been exemplary, but I would suggest that in the future you might employ a little more imagination. You know, Inspector, that if the quality of crime continues at this high standard, I would say that my return to London will turn out to be most timely indeed!'

Lestrade doffed his hat in our direction and then with a final smile of gratitude he turned on his heels and sped off to put his plans into action.

'I presume that you will not be taking any credit for exposing Ashley, as is your habit?' I suggested.

'You presume correctly, Watson, but I would not be too hasty in assuming that Ashley will be so easily apprehended. The powers that work behind him would stop at nothing to ensure his silence and we have already experienced the ruthless and bloody acts that they are capable of.'

I nodded solemnly in acknowledgement of Holmes's grave warning.

'Furthermore, as I am sure that you are fully aware, our work has barely begun. Upon our return to Baker Street I fully expect to find replies to at least two of my wires, each one of which could set a new series of dramatic events into motion!'

By now we had reached the front of that most imposing of buildings that was the Chelsea and Westminster Hospital, and we were grateful to discover that 'Gunner' King had maintained his vigil throughout our extended visit.

'However, we must not make light of the fact that we have successfully just concluded a most testing and memorable case. So, might I suggest some dinner at Marcini's?' Holmes proposed once we were safely inside the cab.

'I should be delighted!' I exclaimed, although in truth it was more necessity than delight that had prompted my immediate agreement to Holmes's proposal.

CHAPTER FIFTEEN

THE DIOGENES CLUB

If Holmes had been expecting immediate replies to his wires, he was to be sadly mistaken. Of course this meant that I had to endure many hours of Holmes pacing up and down within our rooms, while his frustration gradually increased and his temper slowly deteriorated.

To make matters worse, when the wires did finally begin to arrive they were not necessarily in the order that Holmes had been expecting nor were the contents exactly that which he had anticipated. The first to arrive was from our old friend Inspector Gialli and the news from Rome was not entirely satisfactory.

As I have previously mentioned, the fate of both Cardinal Pietro and Father Bettega was hardly what we had hoped for, although under the circumstances, we should not have expected any more, I suppose. At least we had the satisfaction of knowing that Pietro's papal ambitions were now crushed forever and that neither he nor Bettega would ever set foot upon European soil again. Perhaps the penance of their exile and their missionary work would see some good emerge from their sins, after all?

More disturbing, however, was the news that Gialli's assailants were already on their way back to England! Almost as soon as Gialli had taken them off the train and into the custody of the Roman police, powerful forces had been engaged upon the task of obtaining their extradition back to London. The British Ambassador had been summoned at once and as soon as a letter from the Foreign Office had arrived, the two felons were thrust aboard a return train to Paris.

'We must inform Lestrade of their imminent arrival without a moment's delay!' Holmes growled angrily while he hurled the offending piece of paper into the depths of our fire.

'For all of the good that it might do for us!' I complained. 'If the head of the Roman police, who also happened to be the victim of their wanton act of violence, cannot bring them to justice, then what chance does Scotland Yard have?'

'Now, now, Watson, we must never lose our faith in the fact that justice will eventually prevail. Although Pietro somehow managed to escape the ultimate sentence, he will see his current situation as a form of divine retribution that might someday save his mortal soul. I assure you, Watson, that I shall not rest for a moment until our friend in Rome has been avenged!' Holmes vowed with fervour.

'I trust that I might be beside you when you enjoy that success.'

'I would not have it any other way, friend Watson.'

With that, Holmes resumed his endless pacing and I decided to clear my head by taking a walk of my own on the streets below. A dark and swirling mist had been falling rapidly and without warning. Miraculously the streets had emptied and those stragglers that remained began to hurry their pace and turn up the collars of their coats. I followed suit and abandoned my plan of taking an extended constitutional and smoking a relaxing pipe.

I merely scurried to the newspaper stand and soon returned to our rooms and the comfort of our glowing fire. Despite the brevity of my absence, in the time that it had taken for me to collect our papers, three more wires had arrived for Holmes's attention.

Two of them had been in answer to Holmes's inquiries into the Bavarian Brotherhood. However, despite the potential intrigue that each of them might have contained, Holmes steadfastly refused to reveal their contents to me until such time as he deemed it necessary. His motives for such reticence were, as yet, unknown to me, although it was not unusual for him to behave in such an inscrutable fashion.

He offered me the third message without a moment's hesitation and without a solitary word. It came from our friend in Egypt, Elraji, and it produced a change in Holmes's manner that was as shocking as it had been sudden. Once I had read this brief communication, the reason for this change soon became apparent.

It was gratifying to read of Elraji's success in ensuring the continued liberty of Akhom, despite the carnage that the giant had wreaked at Alexandria Station. Evidently Elraji's standing and influence was more than adequate to the task of withstanding the powers that seemed to be following and influencing our every move.

The second part of Elraji's report, however, was almost too much to bear. It was unusual to find Sherlock Holmes so affected by another's misfortune, for he regarded most people and their problems merely as another factor within the complex nature of his work.

However, upon discovering that a man like Shenouda, with whom he had formed a great respect and a very special bond, had met with the same fate as that rogue Hashmoukh, Holmes's Sphinx-like persona crumbled like so much limestone falling into the surrounding desert. He turned his face away from mine, apparently ashamed of betraying what were to him his unfathomable emotions and walked over to and opened the top drawer of his bureau.

We were both fully aware of the object that lay within and Holmes grabbed at it feverously before I had an opportunity to raise my inevitable objection. On this occasion there would be no reproach, for I could well understand the reason behind his relapse. Holmes shot me a brief glance of gratitude and a little guilt but cosseted the small Moroccan leather case within his hand as if he was in possession of the most cherished gift that life could bestow. In a sense and at that precise moment, perhaps he was? He smiled appreciatively before disappearing into his room bearing his treasured cache before him.

I would not see him again until the following morning.

It goes without saying that, when Holmes did finally emerge from his room, his dishevelled and tawdry appearance was no great surprise to me. He shuffled his way slowly towards the dining table and once he had taken his seat he merely glared forward vacantly through reddened and troubled eyes, oblivious to the familiar surroundings.

I greeted his arrival cheerfully and offered him some breakfast, but his response was nothing more than a barely audible grunt. I poured him out a small cup of coffee, although he ignored this, save for when he used the saucer as a makeshift ashtray for the abundance of cigarette ash that he was producing.

He was even unaware of the fact that the flared sleeve of his dressing gown dipped inadvertently into his coffee every time he reached forward to use the saucer, and I despaired of being able to motivate him by any means at my disposal.

Mrs Hudson came and went with the breakfast trays, yet Holmes had barely reacted to her attentions or the awful noise that she made as she collected the crockery together. The bemused woman shook her head repeatedly and looked to me for an explanation. It was not for me to inform her of the awful truth, so I merely shrugged my shoulders and remained silent.

I was certain that Holmes was not only saddened by the death of Shenouda and its nature, but he was also troubled by the thought that had we not made use of the security that Akhom had provided us with, he would have remained by the priest's side and thereby prevented his tragic death.

In my efforts at drawing Holmes away from dwelling upon this very point I began to speculate upon the subject of the identity of Shenouda's killers. This was surely a grave error on my part, for it seemed likely that the source of this slaying would also prove to be the instigator of both the death of Hashmoukh and the attack upon Inspector Gialli. Consequently, while he considered the fate of the men in the brown suits, Holmes's mood darkened still further and he retreated to his chair by the fire.

I tried to draw him towards the windows by making reference to the fog that was now gathering outside.

'It is sobering to consider what dark and dreadful deeds this awful swirling shroud might be concealing,' I speculated while pointing down towards the grey vaporized soup below.

My words were greeted with the same guttural noise that Holmes had emitted earlier and I was on the verge of abandoning my efforts when a saviour arrived at our door in the unlikely form of Inspector Lestrade, and he had arrived with the first positive news that we had received in quite a while!

He burst into our room in a state of great excitement.

'Mr Holmes, Doctor Watson, you will never believe it! We have him!' he exclaimed.

Holmes slowly raised his tired and disinterested eyes in the direction of the enthusiastic detective.

'I take it that you are referring to the one-time valet, Roger Ashley?' Holmes asked, although he had barely raised his voice above a whisper.

'Well, I must say, I thought that you might have shown a little more interest. I would never have even gone after the fellow were it not for you and Doctor Watson!' the inspector complained.

'I apologize, Lestrade, but I am of a particular bent and I will not allow myself the indulgence of dwelling for too long upon my past cases. My mind has now moved on and will not rest until we have established the identity of his employer.' Holmes stated, although he was now slowly raising himself from his ennui.

'Well, perhaps you will be more interested if I were to tell you that we have met with some success with that little conundrum as well,' Lestrade pronounced and with not a little pride.

In an instant Holmes had leapt up to his feet and he was soon lighting a cigarette.

'Inspector Lestrade, I am not so sure that my return to London was as urgently required as I first supposed! Explain to me how you and your men came upon these revelations, if you would be so kind.'

'They were not so difficult to establish as you would have first supposed. We were lucky enough to have already received a most detailed and accurate description of the valet from that indispensable concierge. I immediately circulated this amongst my men and we soon established a network of surveillance around each of the capital's mainline stations and ports.

'As you so accurately predicted, Ashley had no intention of remaining in London for a moment longer than he had to. Sure enough, at precisely nine o'clock this morning, two of my officers observed him on the boat train platform at Charing Cross Station, making his way most furtively and suspiciously along the coaches until he found his carriage.

'My men apprehended him at the very moment of him boarding the train and after very little resistance they soon had him safely in custody. He now remains behind bars at the Yard, although I understand that he has been afforded the services of one of the most successful lawyers in the land.'

'I trust that you have since established the name of his benefactor,' Holmes asked expectantly.

'Indeed we have, Mr Holmes, although I'll warrant that you will be as surprised as we were when we discovered his name.' Lestrade was clearly relishing the prospect of being one step ahead of my friend once again.

'It is always a capital error to make assumptions, Inspector. Perhaps you would be good enough to confirm that the name in question is none other than that of the eminent theologian, Professor Ronald Sydney!' Holmes could hardly contain his laughter as he observed the look of both surprise and consternation upon the emaciated face of our colleague from the Yard.

'Well, upon my word, Mr Holmes, I can see now that you have no intention of ever letting me believe that I can hold the advantage over you. Furthermore, I can also see that you have been holding an ace card all along. Does this business have any connection with your trip abroad, by any chance?' Lestrade asked suspiciously.

Holmes held his left forefinger in front of his pursed lips, although I could sense that Lestrade had no intention of being silenced upon this matter.

'You were in possession of knowledge pertinent to this affair long before you even landed back in England, were you not?' the inspector insisted.

'A good deal, I must confess, although you must not feel overly aggrieved at my withholding this information until your understanding of how things stand has considerably improved. Unfortunately that moment has not yet arrived.

Nor shall it, at least not until my own inquiries have gone a little deeper.'

'Now, now, Mr Holmes, you are fully aware of how the law stands with regard to the deliberate withholding of important evidence. We are discussing a case of wilful murder after all.'

There were certainly strains of the resentment and antagonism creeping into this conversation, as of old. But Holmes would not be moved, despite Lestrade's thinly veiled official warning.

'I am fully aware of that, Inspector, however, I would have hoped that any significant part that I might have played in bringing this business to a satisfactory conclusion might have weighed in my favour and afforded me a certain indulgence on your part?' Holmes asked with a degree of false supplication in his voice.

Lestrade cleared his throat repeatedly as he pondered his next response, and eyed my friend with a good deal of suspicion before he spoke next.

'I suppose that you have been of some material assistance, in this matter,' Lestrade began hesitantly, while Holmes laughed derisorily under his breath. 'However, in view of your past record of favouring irregular procedures, I shudder to contemplate the degree of indulgence that you might be considering.'

'Oh, nothing that need cause you any concern, Inspector, I assure you,' Holmes replied.

'Hmm, well, that remains to be seen, Mr Holmes.'

At that moment a thought suddenly occurred to me and Lestrade's presence, at that precise moment, appeared to be fortuitous. I referred to my notebook.

'Would you mind confirming the name of the pathologist who examined Decaux's body for me, Inspector?' I asked.

'Why, it was surely Doctor Marcus Harding, but why

would you wish to know that at this late stage?' Lestrade replied.

'One moment, please,' I requested and I immediately went over to my bookshelf from which I took down a copy of *The Lancet*. I trawled my way through page after page until I found the object of my search. I took the volume over to Holmes and revealed to him my findings.

'I thought as much! I knew that name rang a bell with me. Look here, Holmes, this man, Marcus Harding, has had a most illustrious career and his list of qualifications is second to none.' Holmes's eyes followed my fingers most attentively, yet he still appeared to have been as confused by my findings as was Lestrade.

'Is there a point to all of this, Doctor?' Lestrade asked with not a little trace of exasperation in his manner.

'Do you not see? A man of his experience and abilities could not and should not have failed to make the same discovery and reach the same conclusions, regarding Decaux's wounds, as I have done!' I exclaimed.

Holmes turned away from the book in a state of intense excitement, although, rather disconcertingly, his exhilaration was tinged with a trace of fear. When he turned towards me again his eyes were glaring with an intensity that was hard for me to behold.

'I will wager that Doctor Marcus is also a member of the Diogenes club,' Holmes declared rather hoarsely.

As I closed the book and replaced it upon the shelf, I nodded my confirmation slowly and deliberately.

'You cannot seriously be implying that a doctor, with Marcus Harding's reputation, deliberately falsified his pathology report?' Lesrade implored.

'I am not implying anything of the sort, Inspector. There simply cannot be any other explanation for his extraordinary findings!' I confirmed.

'What is all of this?' Lestrade snapped angrily. 'One moment you have presented me with a murder case and a murderer that I did not even realize existed and now you are muddying the water again with this talk of incompetent doctors and obscure gentlemen's clubs. I mean, the way you two gentlemen are going on anyone would think that we are now dealing with some sort of conspiracy!'

At that moment Lestrade's troubled features cleared in a moment of sudden and awestruck realization.

'I believe that there is a lot more to this matter than meets the eye, Mr Holmes. Was not Mr Decaux also a member of this Diogenes club and Roger Ashley also recommended to him by a fellow member?' Lestrade began to rub his head in a state of great perplexity. 'Hold on for a minute, Mr Holmes, what exactly did you mean a while earlier when you asked for a little indulgence on my part?'

Holmes approached the troubled policeman with his most charming of smiles.

'I do not ask of you anything more sinister than a little extra time, Inspector.'

'How much time do you require and for what purpose?'

'A mere twenty-four hours is all that I ask of you. If you and your men would refrain from making your move upon Ronald Sydney for that brief period, I will be able to present you with a case that will ensure that your name resonates throughout Scotland Yard for years to come!' Holmes pledged with a dramatic flourish of his arms.

'These are fine words indeed, Mr Holmes, but how do you intend to bring this miracle to pass? How can I be sure that during the next twenty-four hours, Professor Sydney won't slip through our fingers?' Despite the cynicism of his words, Lestrade's manner indicated that the thought of his name 'resonating' rather appealed to him.

Holmes began to coax Lestrade gently towards the door

with his arm draped around the reluctant man's shoulders.

'You may rest assured, Inspector Lestrade, that by this time tomorrow you will know as much about this affair as I do.' Before Holmes closed the door upon the bemused inspector, he had called down to Mrs Hudson for some hot water and a short while later he returned from his room looking much like his usual self.

'Would you mind explaining to me, at least, how you propose to bring this miracle about?' I asked, feeling some-what aggrieved that I still remained as excluded from his plans as Lestrade was.

Holmes lit a pipe and eyed me thoughtfully before making his reply.

'The apprehension of Professor Sydney may not prove to be the straightforward task that Lestrade seems to think it will be. If I were to allow the good inspector and his men to blunder in, as they inevitably would do, then I am afraid that the mysterious third member of the unholy trinity would cer-tainly slip through the net.

'Unfortunately I have still to receive a reply from my brother Mycroft, who has promised to locate Professor Sydney on my behalf. As you know, my brother is normally as reliable as Big Ben, so his failure to reply is of the greatest concern.'

Holmes now followed my lead and turned his attention to the swirling gloom that still pervaded outside our windows. He drew long and hard upon his pipe and the ensuing smoke made it appear as if the fog outside was slowly seeping under the frame.

'Why do you not attempt to locate him for yourself?' I asked.

'Under normal circumstances I certainly would do, Watson. However these are not a normal set of circumstances and my brother is surely not a normal human being! If Mycroft is unable to locate Professor Sydney, why then he is surely not to be located. Remember, they are both members of the same prestigious club and he has means at his disposal that I could only dream of.

'Do you not remember how I described his role within the British Government, during the affair of the missing Bruce Partington plans?'

'Yes, as I recall you said that, to all intents and purposes, he *is* the British Government! Naturally, I assumed that you were surely exaggerating.'

Holmes immediately turned away from his reverie at the window and glared at me reproachfully.

'Watson, you appear to have forgotten one of my principal maxims. To exaggerate is as much of a departure from and a sin against the truth as it is to understate. Therefore, when I tell you that Mycroft Holmes is the British Government you may accept this as the literal truth!'

As the awful significance of Holmes's revelation gradually dawned upon me, I sank back slowly into my chair, feeling both breathless and deflated. The only audible sound that I could muster was a slow and low-pitched whistle.

'Perhaps now you can understand my reluctance to reveal any more than I have done to our friend from Scotland Yard?'

'I am slowly beginning to see things a little more clearly. We are undoubtedly on the cusp of a revelation of startling proportions! Can you not now divulge to me the significance of those wires from Bavaria?' I asked. 'After all, you have allowed me to be privy to so much and I have been your man from the beginning.'

'My reluctance has only been born of my desire to protect you from any potential dangers that this knowledge might bring down upon you. I assure you, Watson, that I would entrust this knowledge with no other man alive that I have known.'

Holmes gave long and due consideration to my proposition,

before making his next response. When it came it was with an intense smile and a steely determination. He strode over to the mantelpiece and unpinned two sheets of paper that he had secured there with a small dagger.

'Very well then, we will see this thing through together, to the last!' he declared before he unravelled the sheets of paper.

'You can see here that this brotherhood does indeed exist and has done so since the last decades of the eighteenth century. Unfortunately my sources are deplorably short on detail, but there is an indication here that the motives behind the murder of Christophe Decaux can be found within the aspirations of the brotherhood.

'They seek nothing less than the establishment of a new world order based primarily upon the foundations of a solid financial institution, under their control, of course, together with science and enlightened philosophy, as opposed to organized religions and other similar institutions. Their membership includes world leaders, leading bankers, prominent scientists and eminent thinkers, who each in their own way hope to contribute towards an improved human condition, but fashioned in an image of their choosing.

'The borders between countries will become blurred while the sovereignties of individual states gradually begin to meld. Individual liberties will slowly be eradicated and eventually opposition to their control will become impossible and futile. Fortunately for us, their progress has not yet reached that sorry pass and we still have an opportunity to halt their diabolical progress.'

'The fact that so many imminent people have aligned themselves to these outrageous aims is monstrous enough, but for them to have been able to operate in such secrecy and for so long without detection is almost impossible to comprehend. I fail to see, however, how the aspirations of such an organization form a motive for the death of Decaux, as you maintain it does,' I admitted, although it was also true to say that every word of Holmes's précis had left my head spinning in bewilderment.

'Watson, everything that we have seen and experienced throughout our travels should have left us in little doubt as to the ruthlessness of the brotherhood and more particularly, Professor Ronald Sydney. The attack upon Inspector Gialli and the unforgivable murder of Shenouda, bear ample enough testament to that! Therefore we can be in little doubt that Sydney will stop at nothing to protect the secrecy of his society.

'We know that Decaux and Professor Sydney were both members of the Diogenes club and also shared an interest in ancient theological literature. The fact that Decaux was a devout follower of the Roman Catholic Church was the only fundamental difference between them. I am convinced that Decaux discovered the subversive nature of Sydney's latest acquisition, the Gospel of Mary Magdalene, and consequently became convinced of Sydney's reasons for wishing its contents to be widely known.

'One of the ancient aims of the original brotherhood was the destruction of the Holy See itself! Although the original brotherhood was eventually dissolved by the Bavarian authorities who had recognized the seditious nature of its intentions, my sources here have assured me that it has only recently been revived.

'What better way to undermine the Holy See could there be than to bring to the public knowledge and to validate a document that will surely challenge and destabilize the Holy See's right to wield authority over the beliefs of tens of millions of people? I am of little doubt that Decaux had uncovered Sydney's schemes and threatened to expose him if the Gospel were not suppressed or destroyed,' Holmes concluded.

'Once again, Holmes, the logic behind your reasoning

and conclusions cannot be faulted. Obviously, a like-minded member of the Diogenes club was immediately recruited for the task of eliminating the threat from Decaux and Roger Ashley would surely have escaped were it not for your sublime talents.'

'Watson, they would have counted for nothing had it not been for the results of your brilliant examination of Decaux's body. Ashley would surely have had no case to answer for at all without your momentous discovery in the mortuary!' Holmes stated and without a trace of irony in his manner.

A few words of praise from Sherlock Holmes were such a rarity that I must confess to having felt a strong sense of pride upon hearing them

'Thank you, Holmes.' I smiled, but this moment of triumph was destined to be a most brief one indeed.

'However, we do not have the time to dwell too long upon this self-congratulatory convention of ours. Watson, there is still much work to be undertaken, some of it potentially dangerous, I would wager, if we are to ensure that Sydney and his subordinates feel the full force of the scales of justice that have so far failed to protect so many.'

Even while he was addressing me I noticed, with some dismay, that Holmes was dressing himself for the inhospitable conditions that still pervaded outside. My look of disapproval had not gone unnoticed.

'Do not harbour any concerns, old fellow, for my venture outside is nothing more daunting than a polite visit to my brother Mycroft's office. His wire is the only one that I have yet to receive a reply to and I merely wish to jar his memory. Remember, time is of the essence and, as we concluded earlier, there is very little of importance that fails to find its way to my brother's desk.

'I promised you before that you would be by my side when this affair reaches its final conclusion and there are no

Reichenbach Falls in London! Would you be so kind as to have your trusty army revolver fully prepared for action by the time of my return?'

Before I could offer a response and with a doff of his hat, Sherlock Holmes was gone.

CHAPTER SIXTEEN

THE FINAL RESOLUTION

IT DID NOT take me long to carry out Holmes's bidding because my gun had been in a state of constant readiness throughout our entire adventure abroad. So it was that I now found myself in a situation that I had endured on so many previous occasions throughout my long association with Sherlock Holmes, waiting anxiously alone in our rooms while being totally ignorant of his whereabouts and when he might return.

My tea tray came and went and yet there was still no word from Holmes. Why would a meeting with his brother take so long? Obviously I could only speculate as to the reason for this delay; I did not have the slightest notion as to the eventual outcome of their conference.

I tried to distract myself by delving into the newspapers that had, until now, been sitting undisturbed upon our small side table. However, there was very little within any of them that could attract my attention for any length of time and I was on the point of despair when a urgent summons at the front door followed by a rapid ascent of the stairs finally stirred me from my anxious melancholy.

I was not entirely surprised to find Inspector Lestrade

standing there before me; after all, he had been very much involved with the case, almost from the moment that Holmes and I had returned home. I was, however, rather taken aback by his appearance. He was red faced and rather breathless and it was several moments before he was able to talk coherently to me.

'Doctor Watson, you will simply not believe what has happened!' he managed to spit out between deep gulps of air.

'Now you simply must calm yourself, Inspector, I am sure that it cannot be as bad as all that,' I said quietly while I poured him out a liberal glass of brandy.

Lestrade drank gratefully and took the glass with him as he sank into a chair.

'Doctor Watson, those two rogues, the ones who attacked your friend in Italy, have just been released and though I am ashamed to admit it, there was precious little that I could have done to prevent it! Apparently, the very same lawyer who had been employed to represent Roger Ashley, Sir Oswald Austin-Simons QC, made a brief visit to the offices of the commissioner of police and the order for their release was issued almost as soon as Austin-Simons had departed! '

I was as aghast at hearing this news as was the inspector at having to inform me of this flagrant abuse of power and influence. However, this was not my only immediate cause of concern, for Holmes was clearly in considerably more danger, now that those scoundrels were out on the streets of London once more. I voiced my misgivings to Lestrade, but to my surprise he did not seem to be in the least bit concerned for my friend's safety.

'That, Doctor Watson, is the strangest aspect of this entire episode. No sooner was I informed of those felons' releases than I received a note from Mr Holmes himself! Apparently, and with your kind permission, I am to wait here with you until a certain individual, who goes by the name of Dave

"Gunner" King, arrives here with news of Holmes's current location.

'As soon as King arrives here we are to climb aboard his cab and make our way to Mr Holmes with as much speed as we can muster, where we shall receive his further instructions. The strangest aspect of Mr Holmes's message was his insistence that I was to inform nobody else of his commission, not even my most trusted officers, save for yourself, of course, Doctor.'

'Yes, that is most peculiar, Inspector. After all, if Mr Holmes is in a position of danger, one would have supposed that he would want us to have met him with as many hands as were available. Was there anything else in his message which would perhaps indicate where he is at present?' I asked while rubbing my chin thoughtfully.

The inspector shook his head and lit up a pipe to complement his brandy.

'He merely suggested that if I wished to be in on the kill, when he does finally confront Professor Ronald Sydney, then I should follow his instructions to the letter. Well, naturally I would not pass up on the opportunity of bagging such a scalp as Sydney's; however I do not understand how he would have found out about those men being released at the same time as I did.'

'Why would you even think such a thing, Inspector?'

'Because the very last thing that he said in his message was that he was convinced that those two would lead him to the very centre of Sydney's lair.'

I thought long and hard before I made a further response. I could not understand why Holmes would have sent his instructions to Lestrade and not to me. Then it occurred to me that perhaps he feared that had he done so, I might have felt compelled to make an indiscreet intervention at the offices of his brother. That was the last location for Holmes that I had any knowledge of and it was probably there that Holmes became privy to the news of the release of Sydney's men.

I decided to keep those thoughts to myself because it was just possible that Holmes had actually asked his brother to arrange for the release of those men, and for his own purposes. This was certainly knowledge that he would not want Lestrade to have and the inspector was only required to ensure that Sydney's arrest be made official.

'Yes, that is curious, Inspector, but I am afraid that I am as much in the dark as you are. We have no other choice than to await the arrival of the cab,' I suggested.

Lestrade solemnly nodded his agreement and we began our vigil. This was made all the easier by Mrs Hudson's insistence that we take a cold early supper, just in case we would not be able to later. Lestrade and I heartily concurred with her suggestion and we made short work of a fine cut of ham, cheese and bread.

However, by the time our plates had been cleared and we had finished our coffees, the length of time since Holmes had sent his message was beginning to cause us both a little concern. We lit our pipes by the fire but neither of us wished to air the sense of foreboding that Holmes's continued silence was beginning to create.

We gradually sank into a drowsy reverie, caused by the lateness of the hour and the atmosphere from the fire, and we were only roused from this by the sound of the dying embers of coal as they collapsed wearily into the grate. Mrs Hudson had long since retired for the night and a glance down at the desolate street below was ample proof that the majority of London's population had taken their lead from our landlady.

The clock continued upon its remorseless journey through the hours and as three o'clock reared its ugly head, I became convinced that Lestrade was preparing to give up the ghost. Fortunately, I would never find this out for certain because at that moment the sound of hooves echoing upon the street outside brought the two of us up to our feet in an instant.

Another quick downward glance validated that the hooves did indeed belong to the horses of our driver and Lestrade and I immediately grabbed our coats and confirmed the presence of our weapons before galloping down the stairs.

'Quickly, gentlemen, for there is not a moment to lose!' King called down and before the door to the cab was even closed, he cracked his whip sharply and we moved off at a brisk pace.

Needless to say, the roads were completely deserted at so ungodly an hour and King was able to move us along at any speed that his horse could muster. This proved to be a considerable one and barely fifteen minutes after our departure from Baker Street we pulled up at a corner barely two hundred yards away from the British museum in Bloomsbury. King then climbed down to explain the remainder of Holmes's instructions.

'Gentlemen, your final destination will be the museum itself, but Mr Holmes asked me to pull up here in case the sound of our arrival might alert the men that he is after. At this time of morning we do make a terrific clatter,' King explained.

'Did Mr Holmes let you know why he had decided upon this particular rendezvous and where specifically within the building he might be found?' I asked, although I was certain that King would only have one of the answers but not the other.

'Why I cannot tell you, Doctor Watson, although I am certain that he is on the track of some very dangerous individuals. He did ask me to make sure that you had taken all reasonable precautions. When I last saw him he was still hiding himself outside of the building and he asked me to direct you to move cautiously towards the third pillar from the left by the main entrance. Unless something has caused him to move since then, he says that you will find him there,' King concluded, and he was visibly proud that he had managed to remember the entire message.

'Will you not be accompanying us?' I asked.

'No, sir, Mr Holmes requested that I remain here as insurance against any of the gang slipping through the net. Do not worry, gentlemen, I also have taken precautions of my own!' King smiled reassuringly as he temporarily removed an old army revolver from his coat pocket.

'Good man!' I slapped King upon the shoulder encouragingly and with our guns primed and steady within our grasp, Lestrade and I made a silent and steady progress towards Holmes's hiding place.

I must admit to being most impressed at the manner in which Lestrade was conducting himself and how steady and true he was holding his nerves together in such a situation. It was I who displayed the first signs of dismay, when we had reached the pillar in question, only to discover that Holmes was nowhere to be found!

While maintaining my silence, I began a frantic search behind each of the surrounding pillars. Perhaps King had misunderstood Holmes's instruction, or maybe we had made a miscalculation? The only alternative to these propositions was that Holmes was now in mortal danger, or perhaps worse?

I lit a cigarette and we stood rooted to the spot while listening intently for an indicative sound. The absolute silence was all embracing and it was hard to believe that we were standing at the very centre of the largest imperial capital in the world.

I signalled across silently to Lestrade for any suggestion that he might have had and I threw my cigarette to the ground in frustration, when a vice-like grip upon my left arm almost caused me to break my silence in shock and a little pain. In an instant I had cocked the trigger of my revolver and I turned sharply around with a deadly intent.

A familiar hand wrapped itself around the barrel of my gun and a hoarse whisper caused me to stand down.

'Perhaps you should save your ammunition for a more beneficial use,' the voice suggested with some urgency, but even allowing for its barely audible volume, there was no mistaking the sound of my friend.

'Holmes, is that really you?' I asked with intense relief in my hushed voice.

Without any further words Holmes pushed down hard upon my shoulders, forcing me towards a crouching position, and he indicated that Lestrade should immediately follow suit. The remainder of our conversations continued in the same hushed whispers.

'I apologize to you both for the extreme, although most necessary, precautions that I have imposed upon you. You must understand that within the last hour, three of the most dangerous men in London have passed through that basement door!' Holmes indicated a large steel door, which was secured with a monstrous lock, positioned within a secluded section of the side wall of the building.

'You can no doubt observe that it has proved impossible for me to gain access to the building so far, and I am afraid that now we must simply wait for our quarry to make their inevitable departure,' Holmes explained, although I could barely stifle a groan as I contemplated a further long wait.

'As we seem to have some time on our hands, would you mind explaining to us how events have come to reach this pass?' I asked with some resignation.

'You must know, Watson, that each obstacle we have encountered, since the beginning of our investigation, has been engineered by the same Professor Ronald Sydney who now lurks behind that door in the company of his equally dangerous cohorts. You will recognize the fact that every trail that we have followed seems to lead us inexorably towards the portals of the same Diogenes club, which is so regularly patronized by my brother Mycroft.

'Even the unsavoury object that I managed to extract from that vile attic, which Hashmoukh managed to exist in, corroborated that notion.'

'Of course!' I exclaimed under my breath. 'You removed a soiled scrap of paper from his table, although at the time I must admit that it appeared to be an object of very little worth.'

'As you know, Watson, appearances can be very deceptive, for that innocuous scrap was nothing less than the remains of Sydney's calling card! We knew, from previous evidence, that Hashmoukh reserved the majority of his ill-gotten acquisitions for Professor Sydney's collection; however, this card also bore the crest of his London club.'

At this point even Lestrade was beginning to appreciate the significance of Holmes's revelations.

'I now understand why you became so alert when I told you that Christophe Decaux was also a member of the Diogenes club.' Lestrade's lips were now as dry as his tongue, but that could not disguise his excitement at this realization.

'Exactly, so who better for me to consult than the man who was one of the club's founding members? I should explain, Inspector, that Mycroft is probably one of the most unsociable gentlemen who have ever walked the streets of London!

'I became somewhat concerned when my initial inquiries to my brother provoked no response whatsoever. Had Sydney already moved himself out of my reach? I wondered if Mycroft's reticence to make a reply had been coerced by Sydney's malevolent power within the brotherhood. My initial reluctance to expose Mycroft to any danger finally became a necessary risk and together we hatched a plot which I trust you will turn a blind eye to, Inspector, once you appreciate the enormity of our undertaking.'

'If I understand you correctly, Mr Holmes, you are asking me to condone the use of your brother's influence in gaining the release of two recognized felons, simply so that you might follow them here to the British Museum, are you not?' Lestrade suggested hesitantly.

'You understand me perfectly, Inspector Lestrade.' Holmes smiled.

'Please explain to me, therefore, what will be gained if I were to do so.'

'Why, it would be nothing less than the apprehension of one of the most dangerous criminal masterminds in all of Europe and I am certain that a promotion would undoubtedly follow should we be successful,' Holmes pronounced.

'Are you saying that, once again, you would be willing to forsake any credit for Sydney's downfall?' Lestrade's narrow smile indicated that he had already anticipated Holmes's reply.

'My name does not need to be mentioned at all!' Holmes graciously conceded.

'There is still one thing that is not yet clear to me,' I admitted. 'Why did Professor Sydney and his men decide to rendezvous at the museum and how did they gain a means to enter the building when you so clearly could not?'

'That is an easy question to answer, Doctor Watson. For many years I have been the principal procurer for the museum's ancient manuscript department and I merely make use of my office in the basement for my own ends at any time of my choosing.'

The voice that provided that answer was of one of the most clipped and modulated tones that I have ever heard. It also happened to be chillingly unfamiliar!

We three were immediately stunned into silence by this

startling turn of events, and we also seemed to be incapable of movement. The sound of three trigger heads being pulled back simultaneously confirmed to us how matters now truly stood.

'Kindly drop your weapons to the floor, gentlemen.' It was now obvious to us all that the perfect voice that we had just heard belonged to none other than Professor Ronald Sydney himself! Consequently we followed his instruction both immediately and implicitly.

'That is much better. Now we can all relax a little better, albeit for only a short while.' There was a veiled threat within the last part of Sydney's sentence that prepared me for the worst.

'You know, Mr Holmes, I saw it as almost inevitable that you and I would one day meet. After all, indirectly and occasionally inadvertently our paths have crossed many times in the recent past. In the end, however, my final triumph has been achieved under far easier circumstances than I could have possibly hoped for.' Despite the tones of his speaking voice, Sydney's laugh possessed a malicious and guttural harshness that belied it.

Sydney's appearance was far younger and less scholastic than I would have imagined. He was quite tall – indeed he stood at only an inch shorter than my friend – and despite his love of books, there was no hint of a curve to his upright back. His eyes were deep set and fierce and the redness that discoloured them told me of frequent intoxicant abuse and many nights of study under a dim light. The teeth, which he exposed as he laughed, were both sparse and malformed.

'I apologize if I have disappointed you,' Holmes replied with not a little irony.

'I can live with that, I can assure you. After all, there is nothing further you can do that would thwart my future plans. Even the unfortunate death of Cardinal Tosca represented only a minor delay. Obviously Cardinal Pietro's murderous intervention, an act intended to both enhance and maintain the dignity and influence of the Roman Catholic Church, was entirely unexpected and did present me with a challenge. However, with the aid of my stalwart allies here, I found a satisfactory solution, I am sure you will agree?

'It was a nuisance that Inspector Gialli happened to survive the attack, of course, but at least he was able to banish my enemy, Cardinal Pietro, to the wilderness of Africa and thus put paid to his papal ambitions. Before you ask me, allow me to explain that the key to my office here also happens to be a master key that afforded me a more discreet exit from the building than you might have anticipated and hoped for.' Again Sydney's malevolent smile exposed those hideous teeth and he now indicated to his men that this interview was about to come to an unceremonious and violent end.

'Allow me one final question, if you please! After all, your current circumstances must allow you some consideration; as you say, there is very little that I can do now to inhibit your future plans.' Holmes pointed towards the three guns that were being trained upon us and Sydney acquiesced with a condescending smile. His men relaxed for a moment and lowered their sights.

'I need to know what fate you have in store for the remnants of the Gospel of Mary Magdalene? After all, much blood has been spilt in its pursuit, some of which has been more sacred than the others, and I would not like to think that it has all been in vain.'

'That, of course, is purely a matter of opinion. At the moment the scrolls lie side by side, along with countless others, within the vaults of the Diogenes club. It is a library of theological thoughts and writings that is unprecedented within the annals of religious discourse.

'As you have no doubt already calculated, albeit with an intellect that is far more limited than I might otherwise have expected, I intend to use each and every one of these writings to first undermine and then finally destroy every one of the world's organized religions and institutions. Only then will a new order, with its basis rooted within sound logic and enlightened philosophy, be possible. It is ironic, is it not, for surely a man like yourself would clearly have appreciated a world governed by logic?'

Holmes merely shrugged and smiled and he then rather curiously and pointedly studied his pocket watch.

'May I just address my colleagues one last time before our inevitable demise?' Holmes asked, and Sydney nodded his agreement once more.

'Doctor Watson and Inspector Lestrade, may I strongly suggest that you BOTH LEAP TO ONE SIDE!' Holmes screamed out this urgent instruction and a moment later we could see 'Gunner' King and his cab come hurtling around the corner towards us!

Sydney and his men turned towards King and fired their guns in his direction. He was moving too quickly for their shots to have had any accurate effect, but this afforded us the opportunity to bend down to retrieve our own weapons from the ground.

Within an instant, King's cab was almost upon us and he opened fire with a gun of his own. One of Sydney's men, who had not heeded Holmes's warning, became entangled within the hooves of King's horse, and the cry he emitted as the terrible damage was done was too awful to contemplate. However, the man's fate was not our immediate priority as Sydney suddenly turned his attention towards us again.

With a scream of frustration he trained his gun upon Holmes once more. His anger and confusion caused him to fire haphazardly and consequently his bullets had no obvious effect. Lestrade and I fired upon Sydney's other henchman while his comrade lay prostrated upon the ground, bleeding and groaning profusely.

The next few minutes are almost impossible to recall in any accurate detail. Events were taking place so rapidly and raucously that I was unable to assimilate my senses within the violent chaos. I was aware of Holmes firing upon Sydney while he, in turn, trained his weapon upon Inspector Lestrade.

The air was full of smoke and the fire from our gun chambers rent asunder the darkness of early dawn, with harsh scarlet gashes. I was aware of King trying to bring his frightened beast under control at the far end of the courtyard, as he prepared for a repeat charge towards our enemies. The animal's eyes rolled hysterically and its nostrils flared with voluminous amounts of steam, while King pulled hard upon its bridle.

I saw Lestrade fall while clutching his side frantically. I could not go to him immediately for I was still defending myself against Sydney and his other gunman. A bullet grazed the elbow of my coat, without making any penetration, and I immediately returned the fire. I stole a glance in Holmes's direction and was gratified to see that he was still standing tall and true within the centre of the maelstrom.

Then it was over.

The stillness of seven silenced guns was as stark as the lack of any discernable movement. Even King's gallant steed seemed to be as stunned as the rest of us and was nuzzling its nose under King's arm for comfort. Gradually, even in this motionless atmosphere, the gun smoke began to disperse and the results of our carnage soon became visible to us all.

Sydney's henchmen had fought their last battle. That much was obvious to me, even from a distance. The man who had fallen under the hooves of King's horse had evidently also been caught by the wheels of the cab. His brown suit was heavily stained with blood and it was now a sorry and bedraggled mess. My last shot in the direction of his comrade had found its mark within the centre of his forehead and he had died even before he fell headlong to the ground.

My services would have been wasted on those two so I turned my attention instead towards my friend. Mercifully, he appeared to be totally unscathed and he knelt down by the side of Professor Sydney, who lay on his back, close to death, but still erratically drawing breath. His lungs had been punctured by two shots from Holmes's gun and his breathing was laboured and shallow.

Even in the throes of death, however, he remained defiant and malevolent. He spat out his venom for one last time, through a bloody and malicious grin.

'Mr Holmes, if you think for one moment that my death will result in the disintegration of our organization, then you are surely a bigger ideological fool than I thought you were. There will always be someone to replace me....' Sydney's eyes rolled back and his head fell awkwardly to one side as his life force slowly deserted him.

'At least I will still be alive to thwart them at every turn. You can rely upon that, Professor Sydney!' Holmes spat out the final words that Sydney would ever hear with loathing and disdain. He stood up slowly and then became aware of Lestrade's prostrate form lying still behind him.

'Quickly, Watson, to Lestrade's side at once! Without the inspector as an official witness, we shall have a torrid time trying to defend tonight's violence to the authorities!' For little more than the merest instant, it seemed as if Holmes had genuine concern for the welfare of our friend from Scotland Yard. Yet it seemed as if even this apparent display of anxiety had an ulterior motive!

A brief examination revealed that Lestrade had received nothing more serious than a shallow flesh wound to an area beside his right rib cage. Although his condition was far from life threatening, it was agreed that King would deliver him to the University College Hospital on our way back to Baker Street.

Once we had been returned safely to our rooms, Holmes despatched the brave cabby with a note to Lestrade's colleagues at Scotland Yard, explaining of their inspector's whereabouts and condition. As King climbed aboard his cab, Holmes slapped him upon his back and congratulated him for a heroic night's work.

In spite of the fact that we had both endured an entire night without any sleep, retiring to our beds was the last thing on either of our minds. The events at the museum had exhausted both our physical and emotive energies, yet the thrill of a recent battle had extended our nerves to the point of breaking and consequently sleep proved to be an impossibility.

As we sank listlessly into our chairs and began to reflect on the last two hours or so, it soon became apparent that we would both be unable to put a voice to those thoughts. It was perhaps easier for me to contemplate the recent bloodshed than it was for my friend. After all, I had witnessed enough death and violence, upon the battlefields of Afghanistan, to last a lifetime.

'What, in your opinion, did Sydney mean when he referred to others that would come after him?' I asked in an attempt at diverting Holmes's mind.

Holmes turned slowly towards me while lighting his pipe.

'It is impossible to say with any certainty, old fellow. Perhaps he harboured delusions of grandeur with regard to his organization? To speak of a successor implies that he was the leader of this group and therefore hoped that he had founded a dynasty. We shall have to keep a very wary eye from this moment on,' Holmes warned.

'Indeed, although I am certain that should we be able to

identify the mysterious third member of the unholy trinity, there would be very little chance of the brotherhood continuing upon its present course. Would you not say so, Holmes?'

Holmes put down his pipe and faced me with a stony silence and a pained expression. As I watched him walk slowly towards his bureau and his abhorrent leather case, I knew full well his intention and again I could not raise a word of objection under such circumstances.

'Sleep well, old fellow,' I called out over my shoulder as Holmes drifted towards the door to his room. His only response was a lacklustre wave of his hand and a half-hearted smile.

As Holmes slowly left the room, I scolded myself for once again having condoned his outrageous indulgence, although this was as a man of medicine; as a friend my sympathy outweighed any fear that I might have been harbouring for his health. Nonetheless, I consoled myself with the vow that I would do all in my power to ensure that Holmes would not be so self-abusive ever again.

I lit a pipe while I strolled over to the window. When we had arrived home a short while ago, the first glimmer of sunlight had just started to break over the roof tops of the neighbouring buildings. By now, however, Baker Street was being swathed in a flood of fresh, early morning sunlight. In spite of this I found myself shivering from the cold and I decided to anticipate Mrs Hudson by lighting the fire.

I was at the point of striking a Vesta when I noticed two balls of crumpled paper that had not even been singed by the previous day's fire. I decided that Holmes had been rather too casual in removing the wires that he had received from Bavaria out of my sight, for that had surely been his intention. I bent down to retrieve them.

I unwrapped them both feverishly, for I was now convinced that the secrets of the unholy trinity were contained within those rumpled sheets. I was to be sorely disappointed. Every word that they contained had been accurately pré-cised by Holmes when he had read them out to me earlier. He had omitted nothing and the mystery of the trinity's third member was to remain just that for a while longer, it seemed.

I was ready to use the wires as a means of lighting of my fire when I noticed a small crest in one of the corners. Next to the crest, which was in the shape of an unusual owl, there were a few badly scrawled words of explanation. According to Holmes's source, this most singular of birds was one of the symbols used in identifying the Bavarian Brotherhood!

Perhaps I had made an important discovery after all, or was my imagination running riot? In either case, one thing I was certain of was that I had seen a similar depiction of such an owl, once before.

That particular owl had been held by the Greek goddess Athena, in a striking landscape hanging upon the wall, in the office of Mycroft Holmes.